Lock Down Publications and Ca$h
Presents

A
Gangsta's
Son

Written By
KING RIO

First Edition 2025

Printed in the United States of America

Lock Down Publications
P.O. Box 944
Stockbridge, GA 30281
www.lockdownpublications.com

Like our page on Facebook: Lock Down Publications
www.facebook.com/lockdownpublications.ldp

Stay Connected with Us!

Text **LOCKDOWN** to 22828 to stay up-to-date with new releases, sneak peaks, contests and more…

Like our page on Facebook:
Lock Down Publications

Join Lock Down Publications/The New Era Reading Group

Visit our website:
www.lockdownpublications.com

Follow us on Instagram:
Lock Down Publications

Email Us: We want to hear from you!

AUTHOR'S NOTE

This book is comprised of parts 1&2 of the original A Gangsta's Son ebook series.

PROLOGUE

July 4th, 2013 Chicago, Illinois

"You alright, son?"

"I'm good. Just hot as hell with this mask on."

"Well, it shouldn't be much longer. That nigga got off work at six. It's almost six-thirty now."

Adjusting my itchy black ski-mask, I leaned my shoulder against the side of Mone's stainless steel refrigerator and gazed at my father, forty- year-old Michael Love, Sr. He was sitting on a crate beside me, right in front of Mone's splintered back door, which I'd kicked in a few minutes earlier. Pops had his trusty old nine-millimeter Glock gripped tightly in his right hand and I was holding my AK-47. Both of us were wearing black Nikes, black jeans, black hoodies, and black ski-masks.

"Man," I said irritably, "why don't we just search through the rooms now? We can find the work and get the fuck up outta here before that nigga get here."

Pops shook his head and stood up. At six foot two, he loomed two inches over me.

"I just did eight years in prison 'cause of three punk ass niggas— Mone, his cousin Manny, and that nigga David. Robbin' these snitches ain't enough. I'ma put the fear of God into—"

He got quiet very suddenly.

From maybe a block or two away, I could hear the rumbling bass in the trunk of Mone's 1971 Chevy Impala. I knew it was Mone because there weren't many banging sound systems in Englewood; and Mone was the only nigga I knew that drove around at six o'clock in the morning bumping Chief Keef.

"That's that nigga right there," Pops said, turning to look toward the living room. "I'll stand behind the front door and snatch him up soon's he walk in."

I didn't say a word after that. Pops had his mind made up and I was rolling with him regardless of how shit popped off, even if we had to kill a nigga at six-thirty in the morning.

"Don't know why you brought that big dumb ass gun," he muttered as he strolled into Mone's gray-carpeted living room.

I studied the dark gray curtains that covered the wide window at the front of DaMone "Mone" Smith's south side home. It was pretty well-kept for a stash-house that hardly received a visit. Pops and I had been scoping the place for nearly a month now, and we'd only spotted Mone's candy-painted burnt orange Impala pulling up and leaving twice. Both times he had entered the house carrying large duffle bags and he'd left without them.

As the sound of Chief Keef's "Love Sosa" drew nearer, I walked into the living room, laid flat on my stomach behind the gray leather sectional sofa, and took a deep breath to calm myself down. My heart was racing, pounding my muscle-laden chest like a battering ram. My face felt hot and itchy behind the ski-mask. I focused my eyes on the AK-47 beside me and wondered if I had filled the fifty-round banana clip. I knew that I had, but my mind was in second-guessing mode.

A minute later, I heard Mone's car pull up and park out front. The music ceased and the car door slammed shut.

Then came the sound of another closing door.

'Damn,' I thought, *'he got somebody with him.'*

***

Lacresha Radcliff was all smiles as she stepped out of the old- school Impala and shut the door behind her. Cresha's rich, brown, model- type frame was draped in a snug-fitting pink mini-dress. Her short hairstyle showed off her beautiful cocoa face. She was a project chick, hustler by day, stripper by night. She knew she'd struck gold a week earlier when she had slipped her phone number into Mone's hand during a late-night lap dance at Arnie's Idle Hour.

"Nigga, how many houses you got?" she asked Mone as he joined her on the curb.

He had his head down reading something on his smartphone.

His Polo outfit was as fresh as the braids in his hair. The small yellow diamonds in his gold Rolex watch were glistening in the warm sunlight. His coal-black face was impeccably groomed and halfway attractive. But Lacresha wasn't admiring his face; her eyes were glued to the bulge on the left side of his hip.

'Damn,' she thought to herself. *'I gotta warn my brother. This nigga got a gun.'*

"This just one of my low-key spots," Mone said. "You gon' have to find us a bedroom set for this one. I only got the livin' room and kitchen set up in here."

"Well, I ain't doing it today, not with the way my legs feelin' right now," Cresha said, glancing to her right and falling in step behind him as he headed up the walkway to his front porch.

She spotted her brother, James' dark green Tahoe parked at the corner of 64th and Peoria. James and five more Gangster Disciples were strapped up and waiting inside the old SUV—waiting on Cresha to give them the word.

They wanted some of that money Mone was so fond of bragging about. The money that had paid for his 1971 Impala and the sparkling chrome 28-inch DUB rims it hovered over; the money that had him buying up to twelve kilos of cocaine every month or so; the money that had his entire click of Black Disciples riding around in foreign cars.

"I hope them legs ain't too tired," Mone said looking back at Cresha's lower half. "You know I just worked a twelve-hour shift. Gotta get me right before I go to sleep." He smiled his ugly smile and opened the screen door. "I'll take you shoppin' when I wake up; spend a couple bands on you."

He put his key in the lock and turned it… but the door was snatched open before Mone's hand could even reach the doorknob.

Lacresha's eyes opened wide with fear as she witnessed a tall masked man step from behind the door and raise a gun to Mone's face.

"Payback's a bitch, ain't it?" the masked man stated coldly.

He snatched Mone into the house and, just as Cresha was turning to run, a second masked gunman grabbed the back of her neck, pulled her into the living room with them, and slammed the door shut.

Chapter 1

Pops started pistol whipping Mone as soon as I kicked the door closed. The first blow hit Mone's jaw and put him to sleep, but Big Mike kept beating him with the gun until his face was hardly recognizable.

I shoved the pretty girl's face against the hallway wall.

"Please don't shoot me," she cried hysterically. "I swear I don't know nothin' about nothin'. He just picked me up from the club."

"Sshhh." I turned her around and studied her frightened brown eyes. "All we want is the drugs and the money, a'ight? Ain't nobody gotta die about this shit."

"But I—"

"Sshhh," I repeated and pushed her down the short hallway to an open bedroom door. "Just help me find the work."

Though my adrenaline was pumping rapidly through my every vein, I could not help staring at the girl's generous curves as she preceded me into an empty bedroom; black curtains over the window, white walls, gray carpet, and nothing else.

I looked at the closet and grinned. The door was wide open, and there were four gray duffle bags sitting side by side on the closet floor.

"Unzip one of those bags," I said, nudging the barrel of the assault rifle into the girl's lower back. "And hurry up."

She rushed to the closet and dropped to her knees, sobbing and sniffling, and unzipped one of the duffle bags. The sickening sound of my father's gun slapping against Mone's head was still echoing through the house.

The girl opened the duffle, dragging it out of the closet; she looked at me with tear-filled eyes. "Please tell your friend to stop beating on Mone like that. He'll kill him," she said.

But her plea went in one ear and out the other; I was far too focused on the cash-filled duffle bag. The stacks of rubber-banded twenties and fifties held me spellbound.

"Old man!" I shouted. "Come on! I found the money!"

"Don't kill me. Please," said the girl.

"Shut the fuck up and lay down... on yo' stomach." I aimed the AK-47 at her face. "Close your eyes and count to five hundred, a'ight? We'll be gone by the time you're done countin'."

She followed my orders quickly.

I was already picking up two duffle bags when Pops walked in. The first thing I noticed was the blood dripping from his gun.

'He probably did kill that nigga,' I thought as he grabbed the other two duffle bags.

I took a moment to gaze at the girl's ample thighs before following my father out of the bedroom.

That's when the gunfight started.

Chapter 2

BOOM BOOM BOOM BOOM BOOM BOOM BOOM BOOM BOOM BOOM

The flashes stunned me. One of the bullets zipped past my left ear and the rest of them etched holes in the wall near my father's head.

Instinctively, I threw my arms around Pops' shoulders and dove back into the bedroom. In the process, through a cloud of shattered drywall, I caught a glimpse of Mone's horribly bludgeoned face as he sat with his back against the living room wall squeezing off shots from a chrome-plated nine-millimeter. Blood was spilling profusely from the numerous gashes in his grotesquely swollen head.

As soon as my back hit the bedroom floor, I scooted away from Pops, let go of the duffle bags, lifted the AK-47, and opened fire at the bedroom wall, hoping one of my bullets hit Mone before one of his could hit me.

The girl curled herself into a fetal position and screamed.

When Pops realized what I was doing, he started shooting at the wall, too. A dense fog of gun-smoke filled the room. Steaming hot 7.62 millimeter shells were spitting out the side of my assault rifle and my arms were jerking uncontrollably, but I kept pulling the trigger until I had emptied about thirty rounds. Then I stood up, ran to the door, and quickly peeked out into the living room.

The sofa was full of holes, so was the wall-mounted flat screen television above Mone's head.

And so was Mone.

Slumped to the side, with a stream of blood pouring out his mouth, Mone was still breathing, but just barely. He had bullet holes in his chest, arms, and legs, and his blood was splattered all over the wall behind him.

Pops peeked out beside me, which is when I noticed the gushing hole in the right leg of his jeans.

"Pussy nigga shot me," he said, touching a gloved hand to the bullet wound.

"Come on, Pops. We gotta hurry up and leave 'fore the law get here," I whispered, picking up the two duffle bags.

"Shit," Pops muttered. He grabbed the other two duffle bags and limped out of the bedroom.

I followed him, feeling more alert than ever. I kept the assault rifle trained on Mone as we approached him.

Pops put his Glock to Mone's battered forehead, and I did the same with my AK-47. We pulled the triggers simultaneously, blowing Mone's brains out the back of his head.

Then Pops and I rushed out the back door to the alley and hopped in my jet-black 2007 Monte Carlo. We snatched off our masks, and I sped away.

Chapter 3

Cresha had let out another involuntary scream at the sound of the last two gunshots, and she held her breath until she heard a vehicle speeding away in the alley. She stayed silent for a moment, praying to God, trembling fiercely. Then she stood up and walked slowly to the bedroom doorway, stopping to pick up an ID card from the blood-spotted carpet.

She looked out at Mone's bullet-riddled corpse and gasped.

"Jesus Christ," she murmured, quickly moving her eyes back to the ID. *'One of them niggas done dropped they ID,'* she thought, not even bothering to read it as she turned and ran to the window. "Lord, please just let me make it out of here alive," she prayed.

Lifting the window, she looked outside just as her brother's Tahoe came screeching to a halt behind Mone's Chevy Donk. Several neighbors and a clique of teenage gangsters occupied the length of Peoria from 63rd to 64th; they were all jumping into their cars and fleeing the area.

Lacresha climbed out the window and sprinted to the Tahoe, tucking away the card in her bra.

"What the hell happened?" her brother asked as she dove head-first into the open rear passenger's side door and landed on the laps of three of his friends. He sped off immediately.

"They killed Mone and robbed his stash," said Cresha. She didn't mention the ID she'd found.

Chapter 4

The bullet wound in Big Mike's leg turned out to be nothing more than a deep gash on the side of his right thigh. While he held a stack of Subway napkins to the leaking wound, I drove nervously down Halsted, gripping the steering wheel tightly and holding my breath every time a CPD (Chicago Police Department) squad car flew by. "Wanna go to the hospital?" I asked, glancing over at him as we passed the Walgreens on 30th and Halsted.

He shook his head no. The expression on his narrow brown face was a mixture of slight pain and resolute determination; we'd hit the lick and all he wanted was for us to get away with it.

"Nigga, this ain't nothin' yo' momma cain't fix," he said. "Just get us home so I can get cleaned up."

I nodded and moved my eyes back to the road.

Thirty minutes later, I parked in front of our west-side home in the middle of 13th and Troy.

My nineteen-year-old sister, Latrice, was sitting in her dusty old Dodge Caravan in the vacant lot beside our two story home, smoking weed with a few of her friends. A group of young boys were lighting firecrackers on the sidewalk in front of our porch.

I laid an old bath towel over the AK-47 on my back seat, handed Pops two of the duffle bags, grabbed the other two, and stepped out of the car. I was anxious to examine the stacks of cash I'd seen back at Mone's place.

Latrice—known throughout the 'hood as "Treecy"—pushed open her driver's door as Pops and I were jogging up the porch's concrete steps.

"Where y'all coming from?" She shouted loud enough for half the block to hear.

Pops and I ignored her and hastily barged into the living room of our three bedroom first-floor unit.

"Assata!" Pops shouted as he plopped down on his raggedy old Aztec-patterned easy chair. He dropped the two duffle bags next to the chair and pushed his jeans down to examine the wound.

I was hunched over the duffle bag the girl had opened in Mone's bedroom when my mother, Assata Love, entered the living room holding Michelle Alexander's *The New Jim Crow* hardback in one hand and a cup of coffee in the other. Like Pops, she was tall and lean with brown skin, and she still had on her threadbare black robe.

"What in God's name are you yelling about, Michael?" She grumbled. Then she eyed his bleeding thigh and shouted, "If you don't getcho black ass off my furniture! The hell happened to you?!"

"Bullet grazed my damn leg," he said, standing up and kicking off his jeans.

While Momma rushed to the bathroom for her first aid kit.

I locked the front door, sat on the plastic-covered black leather sofa, lifted the duffle onto my lap, and opened it.

"Mmm, mmm, mmm," Pops smiled as I grabbed a stack of hundred-dollar bills and fanned through it.

"How much you think this is?" I asked, looking up at him.

"Gotta be at least ten grand in that one stack alone. Ain't no tellin' how much in that bag."

"Michael!" Momma shouted. "You bett' not be in there bleedin' all over my carpet."

Pops chuckled. "Let me get back here and get cleaned up," he said, and headed off to the bathroom.

I got up and checked the other three bags. One of them held seven kilos of cocaine, another held nine pounds of what looked and smelled like Purple Kush, and the last duffle was stuffed full of cash like the first one.

A nervous smile spread across my face as I carried the four duffle bags to my bedroom.

Chapter 5

Three hundred seventy-eight thousand five hundred forty-two dollars is what the loot amounted to and Pops and I split it down the middle.

It was a quarter past eleven when we finished counting the money on my bedroom floor. By then Momma was in the kitchen seasoning the meat for our Independence Day barbecue and Treecy was in the living room smoking weed with her friends.

Pops sat on my unmade bed and stared down at the piles of cash. I leaned back against the bedroom door and did the same thing.

"A little over a hundred and eighty-nine thousand apiece," he said, shaking his head in disbelief. He dug into a pocket of the jeans he'd changed into and pulled out a pack of Newports. "Listen to me, Junior. You can't tell a soul about this money. And don't spend too much at once. Go over to Kisha's house and put this money up. I don't want nothin' here." He paused to light his cigarette. "Just in case the law get onto us, you know? Proper preparation prevents poor performance."

I nodded and took out my own pack of Newports. A million questions were bunched together in my mind like sardines in a can. Could my girlfriend, Lakisha Sanford, be trusted with so much money? And how could I have so much cash put up without spending it? I was already considering getting rims for the Chevy, maybe even *another* Chevy—an old-school Donk like the one Mone had driven.

The most daunting question of all surfaced as I put fire to the end of my cigarette and sucked in a mouthful of cancerous smoke:

Would Pops and I even get away with what we'd done?

"You dripped blood from that bedroom to the car," I said, watching him toss his portion of the cash into one of the duffle bags. "You know they can trace that shit, Pops. Saw it on *The First 48*. It'll only take 'em a few days."

"Well, you need to take care of that. Pay some niggas to burn the house down later on tonight. Give 'em a pound of that Kush."

"You know it's too late for that, Pops. Detectives probably got that whole house taped off right now." I shook my head and sighed. Pops had to leave Chicago; he knew it like I knew it.

Picking up his bag of money, Pops looked at me with the hardest expression I'd ever seen on his face. I assumed he was trying his best to conceal the pain he felt for having involved me in a murder. Or maybe he was worried about the possibility of us spending the rest of our lives in prison. I wasn't sure.

"Let's just celebrate this Fourth of July holiday. Don't spend no more than a rack or two. I want you to drive me down to your brother's house first thing in the morning," Pops said, sounding defeated. He stared me in the eye for a brief moment. "You ask God for forgiveness?"

I nodded my head yes. "Did right before we gave him those head shots." I went to the rest of the money and started loading it into an empty duffle bag.

"When you get a chance," Pops said, walking to the door, "open your Bible to Job, chapter seven, verse one. If my memory serves me correctly, it reads: *The life of man upon earth is a warfare*. Don't ever forget that."

"I won't," I promised.

Chapter 6

By noontime I had changed into a white Armani Exchange t-shirt, black Armani Exchange jeans, and a fresh pair of black and red Jordan sneakers. I put on a black White Sox hat and banged it to the left, a testament to my undying love for the branch of Vice Lords I represented: the TVLs.

I cleaned and organized my bedroom. Then I unplugged my phone from its charger and checked the missed calls. Kisha had called twice and my ex-girlfriend, Alycia, had called once. I peeled twenty-five hundred dollars off a bundle of hundreds and dropped it in my pocket with the phone, grabbed my Glock 33 from the drawer in my nightstand, tucked it under my shirt, and picked up the three duffle bags.

Someone knocked on the bedroom door just as I was opening it and suddenly I found myself face to face with Shay Cooper, a slender-bodied, Indian girl with a caramel complexion that had been kicking it with my sister ever since they'd met at Malcolm X College a year ago.

Shay was twenty-one, same age as me, and she had on a pink and white Polo shirt with matching short-shorts and Pumas. Her soft smile made me smile.

"I smell that loud pack," she said excitedly. "Bust that shit out Lil Mike. Let me get a blunt or two for me and Treecy."

"Nigga," I said, looking at her long sexy legs, "Treecy already got some weed and I gotta go somewhere right quick." I stepped past Shay and headed up the hallway. She followed me out to the car, giggling like the weed-head she truly was.

Ignoring Shay proved to be impossible; she was sexy and slim, kinda like Rihanna, and she always smelled good enough to eat. I'd had the pleasure of fucking her several times already. But as bad as I wanted to do it again, I knew that getting the cash and drugs to a safe place had to come first.

Shay grabbed the back of my shirt as I was dropping the duffle bags in the trunk and she didn't let go until I walked to the driver's door and opened it.

"You make me sick," she mumbled, angrily pushing her palm into my back.

"Why do I make you sick?" I started the engine, pulled my door shut, and then looked out at her. She had her hands on her hips.

"You know damn well why," she snapped. "It's the Fourth. I came over here to kick it with you. A bitch ain't had no dick in two weeks and you wanna leave as soon as I get here. I should cuss yo' ass out." She rolled her pretty brown eyes and sucked her pearly white teeth. "That's why I can't stand your bald-headed ass now."

Adjusting the rearview mirror, I glanced at my reflection and displayed a brief grin. I had shaved my head bald this morning before hopping in the shower and now it was shining in the searing-hot sunlight like a smooth, tan bowling ball. There was a long scar running from just above my right eyebrow down to the side of my mouth, a permanent reminder of the time I'd recently served in the Illinois juvenile prison system.

"Come on," I finally said, opening my door and sliding my seat forward. "You gotta get in the back seat, though. Got blood all over the passenger's seat."

"Blood?" Shay climbed in and sat behind the passenger's seat, pushing the barrel of the AK-47 to the floor. "How'd you get blood on your seat?"

I shrugged and drove off. My mind was still on the money I'd just gotten. The twenty-five hundred dollars in my pocket was begging to be spent. I wanted some rims for my car, some new video games for my PS3, a few pairs of Jordan's, and I definitely needed a fifth of Hennessy to get Kisha and Shay in the mood. But first I had to stash the duffle bags.

Turning onto Roosevelt, I was nearly rear-ended by a green Tahoe; it veered to the right just in time to avoid hitting me.

"Stupid ass nigga," I said as I watched the SUV turn left on Kedzie. "Don't worry about them," Shay said, snaking her head around my seat and pressing her soft lips against the side of my neck. "I should be the only thing on your mind."

My dick got hard instantly and I quickly forgot about the dark green Tahoe.

Chapter 7

"Slow the fuck down Cresha! You almost hit that car back there!"

"My bad, James, I was looking at this Google Maps app. The house should be right around this corner," Lacresha said as she made a left turn on 13th and another left onto Troy.

She had made James drop off his friends before telling him about the identification card that she'd found on Mone's bedroom floor. Now she and her brother were alone in his Tahoe vigilantly flicking their eyes around at the unfamiliar environment. Neither one of them had ever frequented the west side of the Windy City except for those rare occasions when they came to visit their aunt Crystal.

Cresha spotted the house first: 1248 S. Troy Street. There were two girls sitting on the porch steps rolling blunts and laughing. An older man in jeans and a t-shirt was setting up a barbecue grill in the vacant lot next to the house; while a woman who looked to be about the same age was filling a cooler with beers and sodas.

"Pull over and park right up here," James said. He reclined in the passenger's seat and slid a thirty-round magazine into his 9mm Ruger. His coffee-black face was calmer than usual—the calm before the storm. "Whatever happens, don't leave me out here, a'ight?"

"Boy, ain't nobody gon leave you." Cresha parked the SUV one house down from Michael T. Love Jr.'s address and then killed the engine. She held her Samsung Galaxy in one hand and the Illinois State ID in the other, studying them both. "Yup, the address matches the one on this ID, and the ID looks brand new." She eyed the man at the barbecue grill through her side-view mirror. "That nigga standin' by the house kinda looks like the nigga in this picture, must be some kin to 'im."

"Tell me how many faces you see on this block," James said, cocking his heavy black gun.

Far behind them on the corner to their left, Cresha counted five teenage thugs and three adults. *Drug dealers*, she assumed, *out serving their product to the early morning addicts*. A small group of young girls were playing a game of hopscotch on the sidewalk behind the Tahoe, and a brown-skin teenage boy on a bike had just appeared at the corner of Roosevelt and Troy.

"Too many people, James. Too many eyes. We should leave and come back later."

"Nuh-uh." He sat up and peered out at 1248 South Troy Street, then sank back down in his seat and said, "Drive around to the alley behind the house. We ain't leavin' without that money."

Chapter 8

"What's in those duffle bags?" Shay asked.

I glanced over at her and grinned. We were climbing the stairs in the house where Kisha lived on 16th and Millard, and I was having a hard time keeping my eyes off Shay's smooth brown thighs.

"Smells like Kush," she muttered, returning my stare.

I ignored her and dialed Kisha's number on my cellphone as we continued to ascend the black-carpeted staircase. Both Kisha and Shay were from the same northwest Indiana city—in fact, it had been Shay who'd introduced me to Kisha on December 28th of last year—but I was still worried about how Kisha would take to me showing up with Shay. Kisha was the most jealous girlfriend I'd ever had, and I didn't feel like arguing; not now, anyway.

Kisha answered on the fourth ring.

"Come open the door," I said, while my eyes wandered back to Shay's luscious thighs.

"Nigga, why the fuck didn't you answer the phone when I called you earlier?" Kisha snapped.

I shook my head. "Just open the muhfuckin door."

Seconds later, Kisha unlocked and opened the door. Tall, chocolate, and slender, she looked like the Kisha character from the movie *Belly*. She wore a see-through white Hello Kitty shirt over a tight-fitting pair of matching sweat pants, and her hands were already planted on her hips.

She squinted at Shay for half a second, then shifted her accusatory glare back to me as she stepped back to let us in.

"Make yourself at home, Shay," Kisha mumbled vacantly, her eyes burning a hole in the side of my head. "Lil Mike, getcho ass to the bedroom. We need to have a long talk."

Grinning pleasantly, I headed to her bedroom and immediately dropped the duffle bags onto the foot of her bed. She slammed the door shut and crossed her arms over her chest, scowling at me. I knew why she was mad; she thought I had ignored her phone call because I'd been cheating with Shay, a notion that made no sense at all since Kisha was bisexual and would have gladly welcomed Shay into our bed.

"It's not what you think," I said grabbing the $2,500 from my pants pocket.

Her crabby frown flipped over instantly.

"I was busy when you called," I said, thumbing through the hundreds. "Hit a sweet-ass lick for damn near a half million and some dope. Split it wit' my Pops."

"Boy, are you serious?" Her tone was soft with disbelief.

"You think I'd joke about some shit like this?" I turned and opened the duffle bag, then dumped it all out on her Hello Kitty blanket.

Kisha's mouth dropped open and her eyelids ran away from each other.

***

After giving Kisha two thousand dollars and sending her and Shay out to get blunts and drinks, I sat at the small wooden kitchen table with my digital scale, a box of sandwich bags, and a pound of Kush. I dialed my older brother Darrell's number, put it on speaker phone and started bagging up ounces of the strong-scented weed.

"Sup lil nigga?" he answered.

"Loud pack on deck, bruh," I said.

"Whaaaat?" He sounded enthused.

"Hell yeah, nigga. Me and Pops caught a nigga slippin', came up on a nice ass lick. Got me on yo' level now." I laughed aloud, but I was dead serious. Darrell—better known as "Scrilla Man"—was a boss in the dope game. He lived way down in Anderson, Indiana, but his drug ring spanned several states. He had once given me a half kilo of cocaine to get on with, but I'd come back empty handed after tricking off all the money on Kisha, Alycia, and a few other hood chicks, and ever since then he'd resorted to giving me a grand or two whenever I needed it. And he kept track of every dime he *loaned* me.

"Hope you got that ten racks you owe me," he said.

"Ten racks?!" I scoffed. "Nigga, I owe you *six* racks."

"Plus interest," he joked.

"You got me fucked up, Joe. On my momma."

"What I tell you 'bout callin' me *Joe*? Call me Scrilla or don't call me nothin'. And where my old man at?"

"At the crib wit' the OG getting' the grill ready. We're driving down there later on tonight."

"Down where?" he asked.

"To yo' house, nigga!" I said. "Pops might have to lay low for a while. I'll talk to you about it when we get there."

"Shit, I'm in Gary right now and I'm gettin' a room wit' my lil bitch in MC tonight."

"MC?"

"Michigan City," he elaborated. "It's thirty minutes from Chicago. I was gon' come through and kick it wit' y'all today."

I nodded, putting a bud of Kush under my nose and inhaling deeply. "Well," I said, "you can just take him with you when you leave. I really wanna stay in the house wit' Kisha and Shay."

"What?! Shay over there?!" He had a major crush on her. "I'm on my way, nigga," he said and hung up.

Chuckling and shaking my head, I went back to bagging up the Kush while I mentally calculated the dough I'd make off the weed and cocaine.

Thirty-two thousand dollars per kilo. Sixty-five hundred dollars per pound of Kush. Yeah, that sounded about right.

Chapter 9

"Whatever you do in there, James, just make sure you don't kill anybody, okay? I can't be an accessory to murder," Lacresha mumbled worriedly.

James looked over at her, gave her a square stare. Then he turned and continued his undercover surveillance of the house they were now parked behind—the Love residence.

"I'm for real, James. I told yo' ass from the jump I didn't want nothin' to do with no murder. Who's gonna take care of my baby if I get locked up? Who's gonna look after—"

"Shut that bullshit up," James snapped.

Cresha sucked her teeth and lit another cigarette; she had smoked eight of them since the shooting at Mone's place. Her hands and legs were trembling uncontrollably. Half of her wanted desperately to leave without the money, but that was her scared half, the half that was still badly shaken by Mone's brutal murder. What kept her in place was the harsh reality of her financial situation. She was flat broke. All the guys at the club made the majority of their dollars rain down on the girls with big asses and light skin, and the fact that Cresha possessed neither of those attributes put her at the bottom of the totem pole. She was averaging $500 every night she danced, but her many habits—snorting cocaine, popping Ecstasy and Molly's, smoking Kush and cigarettes, drinking bottles of Ciroc every night—ate up nearly all of her income. What was left she used to pay bills and take care of herself, her seven year old daughter Defina, and James whenever he needed it.

'All I need is ten thousand for those butt implants,' she thought to herself as she watched the slender man from the barbecue grill step around the big green dumpster she was parked next to and toss two trash filled bags inside it. She immediately noticed his limp.

Fearing the man would get a glimpse of her face and realize that she was the same girl from Mone's house; Cresha sucked in a breath and pushed her brother's shoulder.

"Hurry up," she whispered, nudging James toward his door.

James pushed open his door and rushed out. He had his gun against the nape of the man's neck a second later.

"Where that muhfuckin bread at, nigga?" James' voice sounded icier than usual. He clamped his free hand onto the side of the man's neck. "I don't wanna have to murk you over this shit. I'm about to walk you into your house, you're gonna give me those duffle bags, and then I'm leavin', a'ight? We clear on that?"

The man didn't answer right away. Watching from the driver's seat, Cresha grabbed James' chrome .38 Special from the glove compartment.

She thumbed back the hammer and stepped out of the SUV, grazing her eyes around the vacant alley. The man spoke just as Cresha made it to her brother's side.

"You must not know who you're fucking with," he said through clenched teeth. "Nigga, I'm Big Mike. *Certified* OG, lil nigga! You better take that lil pistol up the street and rob one of them lil—"

James quickly silenced the man with a pistol-slap to the side of his head. Then he roughly shoved the man around the dumpster and into a small, neatly decorated backyard.

Reluctantly, Cresha let out a sigh and followed her brother. Out of the corner of her eye, she spotted the teenager she had seen on a bike a few minutes earlier, he was standing at the end of the alley with a second teenage boy, and the bike was nowhere to be seen.

The two boys were gazing at Cresha.

She pointed the revolver in their direction and opened her mouth to yell at them, but they took off running before she could get a word out.

Chapter 10

Lucky for me, I'd still had one White Owl cigar left in a glass bowl on the glass-top coffee table in Kisha's living room. I was sitting on the sofa—an ugly burgundy davenport Kisha had gotten from one of her tasteless aunts—smoking a plump blunt of Kush and shopping for a set of rims on eBay when Kisha and Shay returned with the drinks and blunts.

"Let the celebrations begin," I chimed, smiling from ear to ear.

"Look at this high-ass nigga," Shay said with a laugh.

She cracked open a bottle of Ciroc Vodka and poured equal amounts into three red plastic cups as Kisha set them on the coffee table. I caught both of them staring at me as Shay poured the liquor.

'Thirsty hoes,' I thought, moving my eyes back to my phone and scanning the list of Lexani rims. I had a gut feeling Kisha had told Shay about the cash I'd shown her, because both of them were unusually quiet, and Kisha kept glancing at the huge bulges in the front pockets of my jeans. I had $5,000 in hundred-dollar bills in each of my front pockets, and an ounce of the loud-smelling Kush was sitting on the table.

We started smoking blunts and drinking and watching Django Unchained on the 42-inch flat-screen television. Seated between them, I listened to them talk about an engagement ring one of their girls had just received from her boyfriend. Then the topic changed to how "sexy" and "cute" Jamie Foxx looked in the movie.

31

And the next thing I knew, Kisha was taking my shirt off and rubbing her hands across my chest.

"I got my own Django," she said, caressing my impeccably chiseled abdomen. My daily morning ritual of five hundred sit-ups and a thousand push-ups had paid off handsomely, and Kisha was fond of enjoying the fruits of my labor.

"Can y'all please get a room?" Shay muttered as Kisha unbuckled my belt and pants and pulled out my dick.

For some odd reason, she loved slurping on my ten-inch erection in front of other women; and I loved watching her do it. She wasn't all that good at doing it, but she was good enough to get the job done. She'd sucked my dick twice in front of Shay. Both times I'd ended up fucking Shay a few hours later.

I set my phone on the table and eased back on the sofa, eyeing Kisha's tongue as it flickered across the tip of my brick-hard pole. Shay passed me a blunt, and I took four or five pulls before passing it back and asking her to hand me my cup.

"Hope you plan on lacin' a bitch wit' some of this Kush," Shay said, staring at the line of smoke that was curling up into the air from the lit end of the blunt.

My phone started ringing on the table just as Shay was handing me my drink. I looked at the phone screen and saw that it was Tyrone, a seventeen year old gun-slinger from the hood who was always seen riding around on his bike with a big-ass pistol on his hip. I took a fiery sip of Vodka and briefly considered answering the call. But I knew he was probably just calling to check on me, and since Kisha's lips were now jackhammering, I decided against picking up the phone. I was going to whip up a few ounces of hard to give him anyway. Better to return the call when I had the work ready for him to sell, I figured.

I was shaken from my thoughts by Shay's cotton-soft voice.

"Girl you gotta suck harder than that," she said, blowing a stream of smoke at the ceiling fan. "You suck dick like a white girl." Shay glanced at Kisha and laughed. "Like Paris Hilton or some-damn-body. You better suck that dick like Superhead if you tryna keep yo' man, 'cause I can name a thousand other hoes who will."

Instantly, Kisha popped her sucking lips off my glistening dick and pushed it toward Shay.

"Fine." Kisha lifted her head from my lap. "You show me how to do it then, Ms. Pornstar. Give me a few lessons. I might learn somethin'."

I sipped my drink, smiling widely. My phone lit up with another call from Tyrone, but I ignored it and kept moving my eyes from Kisha to Shay and back to Kisha again.

Shay put the blunt out in the ashtray next to my phone. Then she took a chewed up piece of gum out of her mouth and pressed it against the side of her cup.

"I'm tellin' you now, Ki-Ki, I'm gonna have this nigga scratchin' at my door in the mornin', askin' for another fix," Shay warned as she pulled her legs up beneath her and leaned toward me.

She wrapped her hands around the base of my love-muscle and spit on its bulging head, then lowered her mouth and went ape-shit.

Shay sucked dick like she majored in fellatio and graduated summa cum laude. Her fingers squeezed as her mouth bobbed ecstatically. Kisha went to sucking and licking and kissing on my chest and abs while Shay sucked the life out of me.

I dropped my head back and gazed up at the spinning ceiling fan, thinking, *'These hoes is up to somethin'. Or at least Kisha is. Bitch ain't been this nice to me since I moved out last month.'*

On the coffee table, my phone was still ringing.

Chapter 11

Tyrone and his younger cousin Joe-Joe had run all the way to the corner of Kedzie and Douglas after the girl pointed a gun at them. Stunned and out of breath, they stood there for a moment, chests heaving, taking turns calling Lil Mike's phone number from Tyrone's phone—as if Lil Mike would answer for one of them and not the other.

"Damn, Joe. This nigga ain't even answerin'." Tyrone dropped his phone in a pocket of his black denim MFG shorts and pulled them up around his waist; he had a belt on, but the .45-caliber Smith & Wesson on his hip and the twenty-round magazine in his rear left pocket were weighing down his shorts. "We gotta go back and make sure Big Mike a'ight. That nigga had a gun to Big Mike's head, Joe."

"Nigga, *you* gotta go back," Joe-Joe corrected. He was shorter and darker than his cousin, with short nappy hair and a barely noticeable overbite. He, too, wore an Armani Exchange shirt, long denim shorts, a Bulls fitted cap cocked to the left, and Jordan sneakers.

The only real difference was that Joe-Joe didn't have a pistol.

"I ain't got no banga on me," Joe-Joe said. "You ain't about to get me shot up tryna save Big Mike's ass. Fuck that nigga. Ain't he a GD from the south side? Nigga we TVLs—"

"So muhfuckin what?!" Tyrone snapped as he turned to head back toward Lil Mike's block. "That's Lil Mike daddy, nigga. Go and let him know wussup. Tell the Travs too. I'm finna go try to handle this shit myself."

Tyrone took off in a sprint, and was halfway to Anna's— a food and liquor store on the corner of 13th and Kedzie— when he looked back and saw his fourteen year old cousin running up behind him.

They stopped in front of the store and Joe-Joe said, "Man, you know I cain't let you go by yo'self."

Then the two young black boys rushed back into the alley.

Chapter 12

"I'll give you to the count of six to tell me where that bread at, nigga, and you can think I'm bullshittin' if you want to," James threatened. He was standing over Big Mike and Assata, both of whom were stretched out on their bellies on the linoleum kitchen floor.

Cresha had the revolver aimed at the middle of Assata's back and James was aiming his gun at Big Mike's head. Assata had joined the party mere seconds ago when she happened to walk in the back door a moment after James had shoved Big Mike into the kitchen.

"Nigga what *bread*?" Big Mike asked, his tone thick with anger. "Do it look like we got bread around this mothafucka?! We barely got white bread."

"One…" James started.

"What is he looking for?" Assata asked. "Two…" said James.

"Hell if I know!" Big Mike raged. "Three…" James continued.

"Nigga, I wouldn't give a fuck if you counted to six *million*!" Big Mike shouted. "What part of *'I'm broke'* do you not understand? Me and my wife probably got forty dollars altogether, and that's in our bedroom in the dresser. Take that lil bit of—"

"Four…"

"—money and get the fuck out my house 'fore somethin' bad happen. Carry yo' ass down the street and rob them drug-dealers, 'cause we ain't got shit for you."

"Five…" James aimed the gun at Big Mike's left shoulder and slipped his index finger in over the trigger. He was just about to squeeze it when Cresha stopped him.

"Wait," Cresha said, holding the identification card and studying it closely. "Where's your son, Big Mike? Where's Michael Love, Junior? Tell us now or I'm blowin' your wife's head off."

Neither Big Mike nor his woman spoke.

"Try to find the duffle bags," James said to Cresha as he took a seat at the kitchen table. "Somebody gon' die if I don't get that money."

Lacresha Radcliff searched all through Big Mike and Assata's bedroom and found nothing but $42.57 on their dresser. She flipped their bed over, snatched out their dresser drawers, pulled everything from their closet, and emptied two floral-patterned suitcases.

No duffle bags, no cash.

But something on the dresser caught Cresha's attention. It was a picture of the guy from the ID, wedged in the side of the dresser mirror between two pictures of the girl Cresha had seen on the Love's front porch.

The picture that had Cresha's attention was a club picture. Judging from the background, it seemed to have been taken at Club Adrianna's, a popular nightclub in Markham, Illinois. Big Mike's son was hugged up with Peaches, a dark-skinned stripper that recently started dancing at the same strip club where Cresha worked.

Cresha took the picture and slipped it in her bra.

"Hmm. Lakisha Sanford," Cresha said thoughtfully as she turned to leave the bedroom.

She didn't even make it to the doorway.

Chapter 13

Joe-Joe slung the pie-sized slab of brick through Big Mike's bedroom window and watched it collide with the back of the girl's head. She landed harder than the brick.

"Run in there, Ty!" Joe-Joe said, yanking up his sagging shorts. Tyrone ran to the rear of the house and Lil Mike's sister, Treecy,

leaned around the front of the house a few seconds later.

"Oooooooweee, Joe-Joe, I know yo' lil bad ass ain't just bust my daddy's window," she shouted disbelievingly.

Ducking low beside the house, Joe-Joe shouted, "Hurry up and get on the ground! Ty bout to—"

The first gunshot sounded like a canon. Joe-Joe immediately dropped flat to the concrete walkway, and Treecy and her beautiful bow- legged friend Nyomi followed suit.

There had actually been *two* gunshots fired simultaneously from Tyrone's .45 and James 9mm. Shocked by the sudden shattering of glass, James had kept his gun aimed at Big Mike's head as he stood up to inspect the hallway. When Tyrone kicked the back door in and put a bullet in the left side of James' neck, James instinctively squeezed the trigger of his Ruger. Then he slapped a hand onto the tingling hole in his neck and fell sideways to the floor, raising his pistol to return fire.

But Tyrone was quick. He let off four more shots, and every one of them found James, punching three holes in his face and one in the middle of his Bears t-shirt.

"Assata! Big Mike! Come on!" Tyrone yelled, still aiming the gun at the man he had just killed.

Assata got to her knees and screamed, "Michael! Noooooo!"

That's when Tyrone glanced at Big Mike and saw that the old guy had suffered a bullet wound to the back of the head. His cheek was planted in a grotesque splash of brain and bone, and his distraught wife wouldn't stop screaming about it.

Then came three more gunshots.

Stepping out of the bedroom, dazed and aching, holding the back of her bleeding head, Cresha gasped at the sight of her dead brother. She pointed the revolver at the teenager and shot him twice in his left shoulder. Her third shot missed but the first two knocked him off his feet. His gun skittered across the bloody linoleum, and he let out a painful groan.

Cresha ran past him and out the back door.

Chapter 14

"Damn, bae... y'all... need to do this shit more often." I was holding on to Shay's narrow waist and staring at the angel wings that were tattooed on her lower back while she bounced her lubricious pussy up and down the length of my condom-wrapped magic stick.

Kisha was kissing all over the big VICE LORD tattoo that was arched across my abdomen. The pleasurable feeling of her soft pecking lips and Shay's gushy juice box—combined with the good Kush and alcohol, and the knowledge of all the dope and money I had hidden away in Kisha's bedroom—had me sitting on top of the world; or at least on top of the Lawndale neighborhood. I'm pretty sure I was the only nigga in the hood with seven bricks of cocaine—well, three and a half bricks, since the other half of the dope belonged to Pops. Now, sitting on the ugly sofa with two pretty, naked black women who'd been taking turns riding me for the past forty minutes, I was in the best mood ever.

"You gon' get me some Louboutins?" Kisha asked as she eased her head back to smile at me. "The pair I want only costs twelve hundred. They're called the Miss Benin 160 leather sling-backs. *Please* get them for me."

I grinned, grunted and relieved myself into the condom. Shay's snug vaginal walls pulled every drop out of me. Breathing heavily, with sweat leaking down my face, I fell back on the sofa and exhaled.

On the table, my phone was ringing nonstop.

"I'll get both of y'all some Louboutins if I keep getting' treated like this," I said.

Kisha sucked her teeth. "I didn't say all that." She snickered and slapped my chest, then handed me my phone while Shay climbed off of me.

The call was from Treecy.

And the news was bad; terribly bad.

Chapter 15

My brother's blue Escalade on chrome thirty-inch rims pulled up in front of my parents' Troy Street home ten minutes after I did. Treecy had raced into my arms as soon as I stepped out of my Chevy and I was still holding her tightly when Scrilla walked up and wrapped his arms around the both of us.

I had called and told him what I'd heard from Treecy.

"It's gon' be okay, Treecy. Everything's gon' be okay," I murmured, trying my best to remain cool and level-headed.

That's because I had to. CPD patrol cars and SUVs were everywhere. Our front porch was blocked off in crime scene tape. Uncle Mutulu—Momma's brother—had arrived shortly before I had. He was now doing to Momma what I was doing to Treecy, holding her while she cried and screamed her head off.

"Damn, bruh," Scrilla said. "What—shit, what happened?"

"It was some black ass nigga and a girl," Treecy told us. "I saw the girl speed off in a green Tahoe after she shot Tyrone, and I found the nigga she came with dead in the kitchen with Daddy. Lil Joe-Joe took the guns and helped Tyrone walk down the alley to Rick's car. They just took him to the hospital." She shook her head and sniffled. "I just wanna get away from here, Mikey. I don't wanna see them carry Daddy out in no damn bag."

I rubbed her back and pulled her closer. To be honest, I didn't want to see my father's body being carried out, either. But I wasn't about to leave.

Not without my father's duffle full of cash.

I walked Treecy over to Uncle Mutulu's long, black Cadillac and helped her into the backseat. Momma got in beside her. I leaned in and kissed Momma on the cheek, wondering what I could possibly say to console her. Nothing came to mind, so I gave her a hug and shut the door.

"We'll be at my house," Mutulu said as he got in the driver's seat. He had on a gray business suit, the everyday attire of a business owner. He owned two convenience stores and several houses in the Lawndale neighborhood, including the one I was now standing in front of, the one that was now swarming with police officers.

"I'll be over there in a lil while," I said to Uncle Mutulu.

Momma rolled down her window. "That duffle bag," she said, "the one Michael brought in this morning. It's in the trunk of his car. I think that's what they came for. Here," she said as she handed me the keys to my father's broke-down 1989 Chevy Caprice.

'They couldn't have come for the money,' I thought to myself as I watched the Cadillac accelerate up Troy to Roosevelt. And then it hit me. *'The green Tahoe.'*

I had seen a green Tahoe on the corner near Mone's house shortly before the robbery; I'd nearly crashed into a green Tahoe at the intersection of Troy and Roosevelt on my way to Kisha's; and Treecy said she'd seen the girl speeding away in a green Tahoe.

"Shit." I crossed the street to where Kisha and Shay were standing behind my car. "They must've followed me," I guessed out loud.

"Who?" Kisha asked.

I didn't answer because I had no answer to give.

Chapter 16

The following week seemed to pass by in slow motion. Momma was grieving too heavily to manage my father's funeral preparations and Scrilla was too damn lazy—or "busy" as he always said—so it all fell on me and Kisha. The $10,000 life insurance policy covered all the expenses. I went out with Kisha and Treecy and bought Pops a three thousand dollar Armani suit so he could leave us in style—and I ended up on an impromptu Michigan Avenue shopping spree that relieved me of and additional twelve thousand dollars on designer clothes for myself and the girls. I had put Pops' raggedy old Caprice in a local detailing shop for a fifty thousand dollar makeover the day after his murder, and although I was too fucked up over his death, in the back of my mind I was anxious to see the old car's new look.

I awoke at 3:00 a.m. on the morning of his funeral, my head heavy with images of Pops lying dead in his casket, my eyes brimming with tears. I hadn't cried in years, but now I did. The tears crept out of the corners of my eyes and cascaded down into my ears as I gazed up at the clean white ceiling of the Hilton Hotel suite Kisha and I had been staying in for the past two days. Kisha's left arm was draped across my chest, and her face was buried in the crook of my neck.

I thought of the nightmares I'd been having since the day of Pops' murder. They had all taken place in different locations, but the situations had all played out the same way, with me being shot to death while driving my father's

Caprice past a group of young niggas in black hoodies. Twice the daunting nightmares had occurred in front of Mone's stash house, and the others transpired in and around my hood.

Shifting onto my side, I eyed Kisha's beautiful chocolate-brown face and realized why those dreams were bothering me so much: I was afraid that one of them might come true, and that Kisha would be with me when it did.

I pressed my lips against her forehead and pulled her naked body closer to mine. The warmth of her closeness comforted me, and soon I was drifting back off to sleep.

"Lil Mikey. Lil Mikey, wake up."

Instinctively, I dipped my hand underneath my pillow and curled my fingers around the butt of my Glock before opening my eyes to investigate the voice.

I let out a sigh of relief when I saw that it was Kisha. She was standing beside the bed in a black lace Victoria's Secret bra and panties set. She had on the Christian Louboutins I'd gotten her last week, and she was balancing a palate-teasing breakfast tray in the palm of her hand: biscuits drenched in thick meaty gravy, scrambled eggs with cheese, hash browns, and a tall glass of milk.

"Good morning, bae. Get some food in your stomach so we can get goin'. We need to be out of here in the next thirty minutes."

"I'm cool," I said, pushing the tray back at her. I looked at the red digital numbers on the bedside clock, 7:15 a.m. "Just roll me a blunt, baby. And give me a kiss."

"You need to eat something, Mikey. You barely ate anything yesterday."

"I'll be a'ight." I sat up and fingered the crust out of my eyes.

"No, you won't." Kisha planted the tray on my lap. "Eat."

"Nuh uh." I sat the tray aside, swung my legs over the side of the bed, and ran my hands up her soft black thighs. "I'm not about to force myself to eat when I ain't even hungry… unless you gon' let me eat some of this." I kissed the front of her panties, inhaling the mouth-watering scent of her pussy.

"Boy." She leaned down and kissed me on the lips. "Eat your breakfast, okay? I might give you a little snack before we leave."

"Better give me *somethin'*, all that muhfuckin bread I done blew on you."

"So what? I'm wifey, ain't I? You're supposed to take care of me. That way I can take care of everything around us." She slapped me gently on the cheek. "Now eat."

I smacked her on the ass and watched it jiggle as she walked out to the sitting room. We were in a Lakeview suite, the most expensive suite at the Magnificent Mile's most lavish hotel, yet somehow Kisha managed to keep me entranced more than the room's panoramic views. Her sensuous walk held me spellbound. She sauntered the way I imagined an angel would, a perfectly imperfect angel of African descent.

Needless to say, I struggled with an early morning erection while devouring the warm breakfast. Suddenly I was glad that I had gotten away with the cash and drugs. Kisha had started dancing at Arnie's shortly before that horrible day last week, and thanks to the money, she hadn't danced there since; which was indeed good because I hated having a stripper girlfriend. I wanted to be the provider, the man, the pants-wearing bread- winner. And now I was just that.

I finished eating, took a shower, and put on the black Tom Ford suit Kisha had rented for me to wear to the funeral. She had my blunt ready and my tie in hand when I stepped out of the bathroom.

"Scrilla and his cousin Rose just got here with Shay," she said, slinging the black silk tie around my neck. "Rose wants a whole brick this time, and I think your brother said he wants another one."

"Fuck you mean you *think* he said that?"

"I couldn't really hear him with his lips glued to Shay's neck. They probably ran a train on her last night." Kisha twisted her face in disgust as she pushed the blunt between my lips. "No more threesomes with her. Ugh."

I smiled and filled my palms with her soft derriere. "You love me?" I asked, gazing into her sweet brown eyes as she lit the blunt.

"I'll love you when I get a ring," she retorted. "Till then, I'll only like you sometimes. Is that good enough?"

"As long as *till then* you keep bringin' me some new pussy sometimes, I ain't got no issue with that."

"You tryna get slapped?"

"I love you, Kisha."

"That ain't what I asked—" she started, but I lifted her by the waist and playfully tossed her onto the large white-blanketed bed. She giggled merrily, and for a moment I contemplated getting a taste of her juicy womanhood. But then Scrilla and Rose walked in.

Unlike Scrilla, who was brown-skinned, short and a little chubby, Rose was dark and taller, with an athletic frame and an ice cube chilling behind each of his eyeballs. They were swagged out in True Religion blue jeans and Gucci everything else. Scrilla had a big white McDonald's bag folded over in one hand.

"Why y'all ain't dressed for the funeral?" I asked as I crossed the room to a white easy chair. My Mauri shoes were standing atop my two thousand dollar Louis Vuitton suitcase next to the chair.

Kisha's black Valentino dress was draped over the arm of the chair beneath my box of Gucci cologne. On the seat of the chair was my new 9mm Glock, fully-equipped with red laser sighting and a 50-round SGM drum magazine.

"Nigga, we is dressed," Scrilla said. "I'm goin' G'd up to folks' funeral."

"Straight up, G-ball," Rose added, typing something on his iPhone.

Simultaneously, I picked up the Glock, lit the blunt, and threw Kisha her dress. She caught it and put it on quickly... and I caught Scrilla and Rose staring at her as she shimmied into the dress.

"You should wear something respectable for the old man," I said to Scrilla. I sat down in the chair and put the Glock on my lap, studying Scrilla and Rose's expressions.

I sensed bad news.

Scrilla opened the McDonald's bag and pushed it toward me. It was filled with rubber-banded stacks of cash.

"You bring the slabs?" he asked.

"I told you last night I had 'em with me. Is that sixty racks?" I sucked in a bunch of smoke. Kisha squatted in front of me and started stuffing my feet into the gator-skin Mauris.

"Yeah, it's sixty. Counted it twice," Scrilla said. He laid the bag on the foot of the bed and sighed. "Man, lil bruh... we don't think you should go to the funeral. Shit might pop off if some Vice Lords show up at a funeral full of GDs, you feel me? 'Specially since Pops got killed in a Vice Lord neighborhood. That's why them lil niggas got shot up on Ogden the other day. Shit, that's why most of the shootings that done happened in the past week been in yo' hood."

I dropped my head back and blew out a perfectly circular ring of Kush smoke. Scrilla's suggestion that I not attend our father's funeral made me grind my teeth in anger, but I held it in like the next lungful of smoke.

Pops had been a Board Member, the highest rank given in the Gangster Disciple Nation. Yesterday his wake had been packed full of GDs from all over the Midwest, and I had been the only Vice Lord.

Scrilla and Rose were also Gangster Disciples.

"Baby," I said to Kisha, turning my head as she sprayed me with the Gucci cologne, "grab those two bricks out the suitcase, and start countin' that money."

For a while a grim silence filled the room. I sat there in the soft white chair and smoked my blunt watching Kisha as she began counting the cash on the bed. I wondered if my brother thought my hood was soft or something, like we were afraid to show up at a funeral full of the opposition. I didn't give a fuck if every gang in the city showed their faces there, I was still going.

"Pass that good shit, nigga," Scrilla Man said. He walked over and got the blunt from me. "Just for the record, if something does pop off, I'm knockin' heads off for you. But I think it'll be better to avoid that kinda situation... unless you're tryna do forever in the joint."

I stood up and started removing my suit piece by piece, holding the Glock and opening the suitcase. I left the suit scattered across the floor and pulled out a brand new True Religion outfit—a white t-shirt and baggy blue jeans. I put on the outfit, added a gray pair of Louis Vuitton sneakers with a matching belt and visor cap.

"Shit," Rose said, "that nigga ain't gon' need our help. You see dat drum? What's that, a fifty?"

"Hell muhfuckin yeah, nigga, and it's filled all the way up," I said, buckling my LV belt. I knew that Scrilla Man and Rose wore Gucci because they felt the double G symbol represented Gangster, as in Gangster Disciple. So I wore Louis Vuitton's LV symbol for Vice Lord, and all my niggas on 15th and Homan had done the same.

Scrilla tapped my shoulder and passed me the blunt just as Shay came sauntering into the room wearing a short black strapless dress and the six-inch Louboutin heels I'd bought at the same time I bought Kisha's heels. Shay was flipping through a stack of hundreds, fifties, and twenties.

"Here's your money for that Kush," Shay said, handing me the cash. "Fifty-five hundred. If you can hit me with another pound, I'll have it gone tonight. My lil bro want one, too."

"I gotchoo." I was already counting the bills.

"It's sixty thousand," Kisha interjected from the bed. She dropped the two kilos—which were wrapped in clear cellophane and stamped in the center with the letters KR— into the McDonald's bag and tossed it to Scrilla.

"I take it you're still goin' to the funeral," Scrilla said as he glanced from the pistol in my hand to the brand new Louis Vuitton duffle bag on the other side of the easy chair. "Gangbanging ass nigga."

"Hell yeah I'm goin'," I said assertively. "Pops wouldn't have it any other way. I'm ready to die right there in front of him if I have to."

Kisha and I packed hurriedly.

Ten minutes later, we followed our guests out of the Hilton suite.

Chapter 17

"You're gonna need some more dope soon, and I know just the person to contact. This girl I met at the strip club introduced me to him the night I started dancing there. I think his name is King Royce or somethin' like that; a Latin King wit' connections to the Costilla Cartel. She said Royce had been sellin' bricks to the Breeds for fourteen racks apiece. You'll make a killin' wit' those prices."

Lying back in the passenger's seat of my Monte Carlo with my fingers interlaced behind my head while Kisha steered the new chrome 26-inch rims through the west side streets, I was trying to hide the fact that I was still angry about the GDs not wanting me at my father's funeral.

I sat up and glanced around the street—we were soaring down Independence Boulevard—then said, "Ain't nobody sellin' bricks for no fourteen racks. Can't even get *half* a brick for fourteen."

Kisha sighed and sucked her teeth. "Haven't you heard of the Matamoros Cartel in Mexico? I watched an episode about their war with the Zeta Cartel on Gangland. The Matamoros drug cartel is now considered to be the number one trafficker of heroin and cocaine in South America, and a lot of people believe the Matamoros Cartel *is* the Costilla Cartel. If King Royce is plugged with them, then he probably is selling kilos for fourteen thousand." She turned to me with a reluctant expression on her face. "I, uh… have his number somewhere in my locker at the strip club. I can drop by and get it if they haven't cleaned out my locker yet. Or I can call the dancer who introduced me to him. I think I still got her number in my phone."

I shrugged my shoulders and lit a Newport. "I don't give a fuck. Just get me to 15th and Homan so I can check on my lil nigga Tyrone. He just got out the hospital last night."

Kisha dialed a number on her phone and a few seconds later she said, "Hello, is this Lacresha?"

***

There were over twenty teenaged gangbangers posted up on 15th and Homan when Kisha parked the Monte Carlo behind my nigga Tweet's old school Cutlass; the red 1969 Oldsmobile had black rally stripes, black leather interior with red stitching, and a matching set of black 30-inch rims that hurt my pride a little as I stepped out to a barrage of TVL handshakes. The "ballers" of the clique —Tweet, Zo, and Roddy — embraced me first.

Then came the young niggas, like Dre, Shorty Hustle, and Joe-Joe."Here you go, Joe," Joe-Joe said as he handed me a wrinkled and folded knot of cash. I had given him three ounces of crack four days ago for him and his crew to get rid of, and he owed me $3,300.

"How much is this," I asked.

"Thirty-three hun'ed," Joe-Joe said. "Sold the last of that shit the other day. Been sellin' Kush sacks and *boy* since then. Ain't shit gettin' sold right now, though. We just whooped one of the Breeds on Sixteenth. They talkin' about comin' back on gunplay."

Shaking my head, I looked to my right and smiled at Tyrone as he came walking up the sidewalk with his arm in a sling. I watched him and he watched me, while everyone else admired and talked about the new rims on my Chevy.

"Damn nigga, you ridin' on sixes now?" Tyrone said with a grin. "You and Joe-Joe get in the car," I said, handing him the cash Joe-Joe had just given me. "Do whatever you wanna do with that. I got somethin' else for you, too."

"You don't owe me a dime, bruh. I did that 'cause I fuck witchoo," Tyrone said as I opened my passenger's door and slid the seat forward so they could get in.

Suddenly, the piercing sound of screeching tires interrupted the serene street. A white Lincoln came barreling down Homan and two young niggas with dreads and dark faces were hanging out the passenger's side windows with assault rifles gripped tightly in their hands.

My Glock with the fifty-round drum was folded into my seat; Kisha was scrolling down her Facebook page on her phone; Tyrone and Joe-Joe were just getting situated in the backseat.

I grabbed the Glock, ducked into the backseat, and aimed at the rapidly approaching Town Car just as the dread-headed gunmen opened fire.

PHOP PHOP PHOP PHOP PHOP PHOP PHOP PHOP PHOP PHOP PHOP PHOP

The gunshots from their assault rifles were so loud that I hardly heard the boom of my Glock as I started shooting holes through the rear window, aiming at the shooters and ignoring Kisha's frantic screams.

I dove to the floor as they sped by. The pinging sound of bullets ripping through my car frightened me a little, but I rose as soon as they passed and stood beside the open passenger door. I was holding the gun sideways and squeezing off shots at the Lincoln until it made a left on 16th and disappeared.

I looked at Kisha, saw that she was okay, and then checked on Tyrone and Joe-Joe; they were good, too.

But the same could not be said for Luke and two other TVLs.

They were stretched out on the sidewalk, bleeding profusely from multiple gunshot wounds.

Chapter 18

With eight fresh bullet holes in the side of my car, I had no choice but to show up at my father's funeral in Kisha's white Expedition, which wouldn't have been so bad if not for the hot pink Hello Kitty interior. Kisha had stayed home with Tyrone and Joe-Joe; she'd been too shell-shocked to attend the funeral.

I sat in the front pew between Momma and Treecy during the service, flicking my eyes around at what seemed like a million Gangster Disciples and fighting back tears every time I looked at the casket. Scrilla Man was sitting next to Treecy, crying with a straight face.

Halfway through the service, Momma fell against me and started sobbing. Groaning and repeating "No" over and over again until her voice became a small whisper. I wrapped my arm around her fragile body and pulled her close, and we stayed that way until it was time to leave for the burial.

"Walk Momma out to the limo," I told Treecy.

"Daddy's *gone*," she replied weakly. "He's really *gone*."

I nudged the two of them toward the aisle, but they were too distraught to walk alone, so I walked them to the tall oak door, opened it, and stepped out into the sunshine with them.

The first thing I noticed was the single CPD Suburban that was slowly driving past on Roosevelt Road, sticking out like a sore thumb amid a crowd of 400 GDs, 100 TVLs, and eighty or ninety members of my father's extended family.

"Go and tell that old nigga I said bye," Assata muttered, dabbing the tears from her smooth brown cheeks with a Kleenex. "I'm not strong enough to tell him myself."

"You're strong enough to do anything, Ma," I encouraged.

She shook her head no. "Not today, Mikey. Not today," she said, and started toward the limo with Treecy.

I lit a cigarette and was taking my second pull when I looked over and saw Scrilla Man standing next to me.

"We gotta find out who that girl was, lil bruh. The bitch that shot yo' lil guy Tyrone. She *gotta* get murked for this shit. Let me hit that square."

"We'll find her," I said, handing him the cigarette.

There wasn't much conviction in my tone. I knew that we didn't have a chance at finding the girl without knowing her name. Shit, I couldn't even find my own damned Illinois State...

"ID!" I blurted suddenly. "It was my mothafuckin ID!"

Scrilla Man's expression became quizzical. "What?" He said.

But I was already jogging urgently toward Momma and Treecy. "Treecy! Momma! I stopped them just as they were about to get in the black limo. "The girl who shot Tyrone, did she have on a pink dress? Dark-skinned wit' short hair?"

"Yup," said Treecy. "That's exactly how she looked." Momma nodded her head in agreement.

Chapter 19

It never took much liquor to get Kisha drunk.

The shooting had rattled her nerves severely, and now she was sitting at her kitchen table with Shay, Tyrone, and Joe-Joe. They were playing Spades for shots of Ciroc, and Kisha and Shay were taking a beating.

"I quit," Kisha said, throwing in her hand. "I'm way too drunk for this shit. Shay, roll up another blunt. I'm about to go outside and see if that girl done made it here yet. She was s'posed to meet us on Homan before them crazy ass niggas got to shootin'."

Tyrone shook his head in disbelief. "I just cain't believe they came through bussin' like that. We been beefin' forever, but this the first time it came to gunplay."

"Don't even trip, Joe," Joe-Joe said as he picked up the half-empty Ciroc bottle. "We got choppas on deck, too. Wait till the hood cool off, I'm choppin' niggas down on sight."

He turned the bottle up to take a sip but Shay snatched it out his hand before it made it to his lips.

"You too young to be drinkin'," Shay said, filling her shot glass with the vodka. "Two shots is enough for you."

"Fuck you think you talkin' to? I'm fourteen goin' on thirty, and I got a grown man dick and a grown man bankroll..."

Joe-Joe was flaunting a stack of cash in Shay's face when Tyrone got up and followed Kisha out of the kitchen.

"I'm not lettin' you go outside drunk like this," Tyrone said, grabbing ahold of Kisha's elbow just as they were entering the living room. "Wait till Mikey get back. You can't even walk straight right now."

"Boy you better let me go before you end up wit' *two* useless arms." She yanked her elbow out of his grasp. "I'm good, okay? Shit, I might be able to get this hoe to give you some pussy. She a stripper, dark like me, kinda cute, too."

Shaking his head, and secretly scoping Kisha's plump backside, he locked his fingers around her elbow again. But this time he pushed her onto the new white leather sofa.

She looked up at him and laughed. Her eyes drifted down to the crotch of his jeans and she reached out to touch it; he slapped her hand so hard that she snatched it back and massaged it.

Tyrone's expression became a mask of disgust. He was attracted to Kisha the same way he was to all beautiful black women, but his loyalty to Mikey and the TVL mob came first.

"You ain't *that* muhfuckin drunk," he said, scowling.

"I know." Kisha shook her head. "I'm sorry, Tyrone. I'm so fucked up off that Ciroc." She reached around him and lifted her phone from the table. "Damn, Cre done called me three times already."

"Who?"

"Lacresha, the stripper I was just tellin' you about, the one who was supposed to meet us on Homan when they started shootin'."

Tyrone frowned thoughtfully.

Kisha returned Lacresha's call.

Chapter 20

In the alley a block down from Kisha's Millard Street home, Lacresha drove up beside the white Lincoln and parked. She was behind the wheel of her new friend King-Royce's shiny yellow Bentley coupe. A dark pair of Chanel shades shielded her blood-shot eyes from the harsh sunlight and her tiny, yellow, one-shouldered Prada dress left little to the imagination. Yesterday she had watched her brother's casket get lowered into the earth, and then she had driven home to Royce's condo in his black Benz and curled up in bed alone, crying her eyes out and reading a LaTonya West novel on her iPad's Kindle app.

Royce had stayed at the small mansion that he shared with his wife Aesha in Bellwood, just as he'd been doing since he'd given Cresha the keys to his Gold Coast condo. She knew he was only helping her out of sympathy; She was his favorite stripper at Arnie's, had been for months, plus she and James had just bought nine ounces of soft from Royce a couple of weeks ago, and eight pounds of Kush a month before that.

Cresha took a seven gram bag of coke out of her Coach bag and poured a little onto the screen of her iPad. The Bentley's passenger door opened and in climbed two dark-hued goons, both with assault rifles gripped tightly in their veiny teenaged hands. Branches of dread locks were draped over their cold young eyes.

"Please," Cresha said, rolling a hundred dollar bill into a nose straw, "tell me y'all found that nigga and put a hole in his head."

"We aired out the whole block. The whip we been seein' outside ol' girl crib was out there. We wet that muhfucka up, too," said Treys, the violently-composed Black Disciple in the passenger's seat. "A nigga in that Monte Carlo got to bussin' back and shot Lil Bobo in the neck. Lil nigga in there bleedin' out as we speak."

"Hell yeah," said Two-One, the BD who was sitting behind Treys. "That lil nigga stretched out in the backseat lookin' paler than a muhfucka. He called his momma. She on her way to get him now."

Cresha snorted up a line of coke and then dropped her head back, pinching the bridge of her nose between her two fingers. *'These lil nigga gon' get me locked up,'* she thought to herself before glancing over at the white Lincoln.

"Does she know that he was with y'all?"

Treys shook his head no. "Fuck is we still sittin' here for? Let's ride, nigga." He reclined his seat and waited for her to pull off.

But Cresha didn't step her Prada heel on the gas pedal. She snorted up another line of uncut powder then dug in her purse and, ignoring her vibrating phone, pulled out the chrome .38 she had gotten from her brother, and handed it to Treys.

"Y'all just put in some serious work for me, and I'm not tryna be tied up in court over this shit." Cresha locked eyes with the young goon sitting next to her. "Think they ain't gon' question Bobo when he get to the hospital? You better handle that shit 'fore we end up wit' life sentences."

"Hell muhfuckin yeah," Two-One agreed from the backseat. "We just met that lil nigga anyway. If he fold, we all fucked."

Aggressively, Treys pushed open his door and walked over to the old white Lincoln. He stuck the revolver through the driver's side window and two thunderous gunshots followed.

Cresha watched the blood splash up onto the rear windows. Then Treys returned to his seat in the Bentley and Cresha sped off.

Chapter 21

"I miss you already, Pops," I said, standing beside the casket with my brother. "Guess I'll see you again one day. I know I will. And I hope shit get a lil better after this life."

"Straight up," Scrilla Man said. "Ain't never gon' be another nigga like you. Wish I wouldn't have stayed out of town so much. I was s'posed to be there to burn that nigga who shot you."

Shaking my head despondently, I leaned closer to my father's misshapen face and whispered, "It was my ID, Pops. I dropped my ID in that bedroom, and that girl picked it up when we left."

Scrilla Man gave me a questioning look, so I stepped aside and explained how the robbery had transpired, while a steady line of old-school gangsters, pimps, young thugs, and family members stepped up and paid their last respects to Pops.

"Man," Scrilla said when I was done telling him about the robbery. He lifted his eyes to a statue of Jesus hanging from a cross. "I hate to say it, but we can't let ol' girl get away wit' this. If she brought a nigga to rob you once, she'll do it again. Guarantee it."

"I already know, bruh." I glanced over at Jessica, a thickly built redbone who was sauntering toward us in a snug-fitting white dress. She was an eighteen year old hood chick off 16th and Spaulding, brought to the funeral by her father, Big Cory, who had been tight with Pops for decades.

"Where you gon' be after the funeral?" She asked me.

"At the cemetery." I checked my phone for the time. "Why?"

"Cause Sicko Mob got a video shoot on Christiana tonight."

"I ain't gon' miss it," I said.

"Can you pick me up from my auntie crib on Lawndale at seven? I gotta babysit my nephews till six-thirty, and I don't wanna walk all the way down there wit' all the shootin' that's been goin' on."

"I gotchoo. Just call and remind me at around—"

My words ceased at the sight of Manny, Mone's cousin. He was walking up to the casket in a fresh gray suit that matched the graying braids on his coal black scalp. He had tears sliding down his face.

"First Mone, now you," Manny said, sniffling.

He didn't get another word out. I turned and broke his jaw with a vicious right haymaker and he collapsed to the floor, unconscious and bleeding from the mouth. I managed to stomp his face twice and snatch the Glock from my waist before Scrilla Man wrapped his powerful arms around me, lifted me into the air, and carried me a good ten feet away.

Quickly regaining my composure, I ripped loose and put the gun back on my hip. "That nigga snitched on Pops!" I was furious… until I noticed that several of my aunts, uncles, and cousins were scurrying out of the church with their children, while the Gangsters gazed down at Manny's sleeping body with amusement etched on their black faces.

Rose kicked the side of Manny's head and spit on his forehead as we were leaving.

We decided against attending the burial. Instead, I hopped in Kisha's SUV, hardly noticing Jessica's presence as she slid into the passenger's seat beside me. I sped off ahead of Scrilla's Escalade.

"Why did you knock that man out like that?" Jessica asked. She sighed and studied the AK-47 that was lying between our seats. "You're crazy, you now that? All of you niggas off fifteenth—y'all get money, but y'all get crazy, too. I was right around the corner on Trumbull when y'all got to shootin' earlier. Lil Will's momma said he might not pull through." She sucked her teeth indignantly and mumbled, "I bet it was them Breeds off thirteenth and Christiana."

I lit a cigarette and was silent for a moment as I drove down Douglas Boulevard. My eyes flicked to and fro, searching for the white Lincoln I'd shot at earlier. I spotted numerous cars full of TVLs driving around aimlessly and I knew that they, too, were searching for the Lincoln.

"Where you wanna get dropped off at?" I said finally.

"I'll walk from Kisha's house." Jessica was twirling a lock of her long black hair around the tip of a perfectly manicured and polished forefinger. She was a certified dime piece, short and pretty with a body like K. Michelle's. "Or y'all can come kick it wit' me and my bitches," she added, blowing a big pink bubble with the gum she was chewing.

I decided the latter suggestion was more reasonable.

Chapter 22

"Lay down and take a nap, Kisha. You are way too fucked up," Tyrone said as he laid Kisha on her bed and covered her with a blanket. He and Joe-Joe had just carried her from the bathroom after watching her vomit out everything she'd eaten.

Kisha turned over to face Tyrone as Joe-Joe was leaving the bedroom. She laughed abruptly when the door clicked shut.

"Ain't shit funny," Tyrone said, taking a seat next to her. He checked his phone to see if his girlfriend had called yet.

She hadn't.

"Nothin' ass bitch," Tyrone spat, setting the phone aside. He leaned forward and adjusted the sling on his arm, wondering where the two gunshots they'd heard a few minutes ago had come from. The feeling of Kisha's hand caressing his lower back pulled him away from his thoughts. "Stop touchin' me, Kisha."

"Boy, do I look like I'm touchin' you?"

"I'm dead serious."

"I am, too," Kisha said, still rubbing his back.

Just then his phone rang. It was Mikey.

Tyrone knocked Kisha's hand away and stood up to answer the call. She smiled, eyeing the bulging front of his pants.

"Man, I done whooped a nigga at the funeral," Mikey said. "We ain't goin' to the burial. I'm over Sandy crib now.

'Bout to fuck lil thick-ass Jessica then slide over there to pick y'all up. Shit, nigga, you see all them police cars in the alley? I think somebody got whacked back there."

"Nah, I ain't even looked." Tyrone was grinding his teeth together, and his nostrils were flaring.

"Just sit tight, lil bruh. I got a few more blessin's for you. Finna buss lil momma down first. On King James I got you, though."

"Yup," was Tyrone's brief reply.

He ended the call and leaned forward against the side of the bed. Kisha reached out and touched the hard pole that was hidden in his jeans. This time she received no resistance. Tyrone stared down at her hand as she squeezed and tugged on his erection, and he didn't say a word when she unbuckled his Louis Vuitton belt, pulled his dick out, and started jerking it back and forth.

"Lock the door and lay down right here," Kisha said, scooting over and slapping the center of the bed.

Tyrone did as he was told.

Seconds later, he was lying in bed with his pants and boxers pushed down around his knees. Kisha licked and sucked his dick for a nice long while, and he didn't feel bad at all.

Because Tyrone's girlfriend was Jessica, though Mikey didn't know it.

Chapter 23

"Where da money you owe us at?" Treys asked, turning to Cresha with the revolver in hand.

She pointed at a box of Kleenex tissues on the dashboard. "It's in there, under the tissue. Four racks, all hundreds." She sucked her teeth and added, "I shouldn't have to pay you niggas nothin'. It ain't like y'all killed who I sent y'all to kill. Nah, you blind mothafuckas went and shot everybody *but* him."

"You paid us to ride down on the niggas that killed James. We did that," Treys retorted.

Two-One stuck his head in between the front seats to watch Treys count the money, and Cresha's eyes returned to the road ahead. She had stopped in another alley just long enough for the young thugs to stash their assault rifles in the trunk. Now she was cruising down Roosevelt Road with the tinted windows up and the AC blasting. She put on a shocked expression every time a CPD vehicle sped by.

Her mind was on her money. After selling her brother's SUV and the few ounces of coke he'd left in her attic, Cresha had ended up with a little over $8,500; now she was down to $4,500, and she wasn't happy about it. In fact, she was so *unhappy* about it that she started crying.

"Maaaan," Treys said, counting the money again, "don't start wit' that shit on us. We really wanted to get at them niggas for killin' Mone, and we aired out that Monte Carlo, too. We gave 'em the *b'ness*. Fuck is you cryin' about? You can stop that bull—"

SKEEEERK!

The Bentley's tires screamed as Cresha busted a sudden U-turn in the middle of traffic, nearly crashing her rear bumper against the front end of an F-150 pick-up truck.

Two-One leaned forward and pressed the barrel of his 30-round Ruger pistol against her cheek. "Bitch, what the fuck you on?! Get us back to Englewood ASAP!"

"Chill out, bruh," Treys said, grabbing Two-One's wrist and forcing him to lower the weapon. "We'll go back. But on David, if somethin' happens to us, my lil shooters gon' tear yo' whole family up."

Wiping away her tears, Cresha stepped on the gas.

Chapter 24

The wet sounds Jessica's pussy made at my every thrust was like music to my ears. Kneeling behind her on an air mattress in her aunt, Sandy's, daughter's bedroom, I was gripping her hips and pounding in and out of her while she worked her mouth up and down my brother's dick.

On the side of the mattress, Rose was fucking Makayla, a cute brown-skin girl. A few blunts of Kush was all it had taken to get them to buss down, and I wanted to enjoy every minute of it. After all that had happened in the past week, it felt good to be dicking down a thick bad bitch. I wanted the feeling to last forever.

I took off the condom, traded places with Scrilla, and palmed the back of Jessica's head until I filled her mouth with semen.

That is when the banging started.

THUMP THUMP THUMP THUMP THUMP THUMP THUMP

It sounded like someone was trying to punch through the front door. "Who the fuck is that?" Rose asked.

I dressed hurriedly and stepped out into the dingy living room; Scrilla and Rose were seconds behind me, fastening their jeans and belts.

Jessica's other friend—a pregnant chubby girl named Stacy—was peeking out the window with a shocked expression on her plump black face.

The banging continued. "Who out there?" I asked.

"Makayla's boyfriend," Stacy answered. "That nigga Ton from off Trumbull. He gon' whoop Makayla's ass for bein' in here with y'all."

Jessica and Makayla came out of the bedroom wrapped in bed sheets. Makayla looked scared.

"Y'all go out the back door," she said.

"What?!" I said, walking to the front door. "This soft ass nigga ain't gon' do nothin'."

I opened the door and stared Ton down. He was taller than me and about a hundred pounds heavier.

"Makayla, getcho ass out here!" Ton snapped as he attempted to push me aside.

Wrong move.

I hit him with five sharp jabs, and before he could turn to defend himself, Scrilla Man and Rose were flooding his face with punches.

We knocked him to the floor and stomped him to sleep. Makayla tried intervening and caught an accidental elbow to the jaw from Rose. Scrilla Man picked up a closed baby stroller that was leaning against the wall and started beating Ton's head with it.

Then Scrilla Man and Rose finished getting dressed and we left.

Chapter 25

"Mmm, shit, I'm finna cum," Tyrone said, holding on to Kisha's waist with his one good hand as she rode him reverse cowgirl style.

She tightened her vaginal muscles around his bare dick and slowed down a bit, squeezing the cum out of him until his twitching pole dropped from inside her and collapsed onto his abdomen.

She moved forward on her hands and knees so that her glistening wet pussy was directly over his deflating manhood. She pushed his semen out, and it dripped down onto the shaft of his dick.

"Damn," was all he could say as Kisha turned around and sucked the cum into her mouth.

"You like that shit, don't you?" she asked, swallowing his seed.

Tyrone responded with a short, breathless laugh. He watched her pull the tight black dress down and search around for her panties, while he yanked up his boxers and pants. When they opened the bedroom door, Shay and Joe-Joe were standing there in the hallway with knowing smirks on their faces.

"Fuck is y'all smilin' about?" Tyrone snapped.

Shay crossed her arms over her small chest and slowly nodded her head. "Mmmm hmmm. We saw it all through the keyhole."

"Y'all ain't seen shit." Tyrone stepped around them and was just about to go in the bathroom to clean himself up when suddenly the front door swung open.

***

I looked at Tyrone and smiled as I walked through the door. "Just drove past the alley," I said. "They pullin' a body out that white Lincoln. Police everywhere."

"Shit," said Joe-Joe, "you already knew dat was gon' happen. Them weak ass Breeds ain't got shit on us. Lucky it wasn't *me* that caught up wit' em. On God, Joe, I would've—"

Joe-Joe went silent as I squinted at Kisha, Tyrone, and Shay; the three of them were following Joe-Joe into the living room, and they all seemed tense and unusually quiet.

"What's wrong?" I asked no one in particular.

"Ain't nothin' wrong," Shay said.

But I still felt an odd tension in the air as I joined Rose and Scrilla Man on the new sofa. I shook it off and pulled Kisha down onto my lap, then started telling Tyrone how we had just stomped Ton's lights out. Kisha got up and headed toward the bathroom before I could finish explaining the situation.

"Where the hell you goin'?" I shouted.

"To brush my teeth," Kisha replied. "I threw up a few minutes ago.

You don't want me kissin' you wit' throw up all on my tongue, do you?"

'Drunk-ass light-weight,' I thought, turning back to Tyrone.

"I'm takin' you car shoppin' tomorrow," I said, lighting a cigarette. "Find you a nice ol' school 'Lac or Chevy. I got some dope and some Kush for you, too. A whole brick and a pound."

"Damn, for real?" Tyrone rubbed his hands together.

"Lil nigga, I owe you more than that," I said, picking up Kisha's ringing phone from the coffee table.

Somebody named Lacresha was calling. I answered the call.

"Hello?" Silence.

"Hello?" I repeated.

"Is, um…is Kisha there?" A girl asked.

"Yeah. Hold on a minute."

Kisha returned a moment later and I handed her the phone. I massaged her soft thighs and hoped she would not catch the lingering scent of Jessica's perfume as she lifted the phone to her ear.

"Hey, Bitch. Where you at? Bitch, I done got *wasted* waitin' on yo' ass to show up…"

I moved from beneath Kisha and stood up, mostly because I didn't want to argue with her if her nose got nosey like it sometimes did, but also because I wanted to give Tyrone the paper bag I had ready for him in the bedroom.

To Kisha, I muttered, "You startin' to drink too muhfuckin much… and stop thinkin' you got so many friends."

She sucked her teeth and twisted her face at me. I continued up the hallway ahead of Tyrone, adjusting the bulging pistol on my hip and checking my phone. My mother and sister were blowing me up with texts and calls, and so were a dozen other family members. I wasn't about to reply to any of them; at least not now, when my father's body was lying in a freshly dug grave. Not while four of my mob brothers were stretched out in hospital beds with bodies full of bullet holes.

I put the phone back on my hip as we entered the bedroom. The strong smell of sex struck me immediately.

I looked up at Tyrone and grinned as I squatted and grabbed the large paper bag from under the bed.

"You fucked Shay, didn't you?" I asked.

He grinned with me. "And you fucked Jessica, didn't you? We even." He accepted the bag, opened it, and peered inside. His grin blossomed into a full-blown smile. "Shit, that's thirty-six zips? A whole brick? *And* a pound of *Kush*?" He was in shock.

"You don't owe me a dime, either. Just come back and shop wit' me.

I should be on again within the next few days."

"We'll get rich together, then. I'm wit' it."

"Well, that's what it is," I said, demonstrating the TVL handshake with him. "Get money to the death of us."

"On King James," he replied.

The next thing I knew, Shay was screaming at the top of her lungs.

Chapter 26

"MIKEY! MIKEY, THEY'RE TAKING KISHA!"

I rushed out to the living room just as everyone was running out the door. I ran down the front stairs behind Shay, with Tyrone right in back of me.

"I saw it from the window," Shay said frantically. "Some nigga put a gun to her head and made her get in the trunk of a yellow Bentley."

The six of us made it to the porch in time to see the Bentley veering around the corner on 16th Street.

"Shit, come on y'all!" I yelled, sprinting towards Kisha's SUV. But it was to no avail.

By the time I made it to 16th, the Bentley was gone.

We drove around for nearly an hour, through all the side and main streets, past hundreds of black civilians and dozens of white policemen, gangbangers and drug dealers.

Still, no sign of the Bentley.

"We need to go back to the house," Joe-Joe said from behind me. "Kisha left her phone on the table. I think she was waitin' on somebody."

"Yup," Tyrone said, nodding his head in agreement. He was sitting in the passenger's seat with the paper bag on his lap. "She was waitin' on some stripper bitch. I can't remember the bitch's name."

Seeing the paper bag brought me back to reality: we were riding around with a kilo of coke and a pound of Kush, and there were two kilos in Scrilla Man's SUV.

As we were stopping at a traffic light on 16th, I pulled up alongside the Escalade and rolled my window down. Rose rolled down his window, too.

"Y'all go on back to Indiana wit' that shit." I sighed and lit a cigarette, glancing at a cop car in my rearview mirror.

"*Hell* muhfuckin naw," Scrilla Man said. "We gon' handle all this shit first, lil bruh."

Back to back, we returned to Kisha's house.

Chapter 27

A warm stream of urine snaked its way around Kisha's right thigh, wetting the side of her dress. She was sobbing uncontrollably in the dark confines of the trunk, asking herself a thousand questions.

'How long have I been in here? Where are they taking me? Shit, did anybody even see what happened?'

"God, please don't let them kill me," she cried. "Lord Jesus, please save me. I know I've done a lot of sinning, but don't let me die today. I'll change. I swear I'll change right now."

She yelped as the car hit a bump. Something hard and sharp hit her forehead. Ignoring the painful stinging sensation, she reached up and curled her fingers around the object.

A crowbar?

Yes, it definitely was a crowbar.

She grabbed it and was just about to try prying the trunk open when she remembered seeing a pair of assault rifles before the gunman had slammed the trunk shut.

***

"We need to hurry up and get dat bitch out the trunk. She back there wit' dem choppas," Treys said.

"Boy, don't start gettin' on my damn nerves. We're almost there. Shut the hell up and let me drive," Cresha snapped.

Lacresha was aggravated for a number of reasons. For one, she was almost flat broke; and for two, she was now being hounded by a homicide detective that had already visited the strip club where she danced twice.

Evidently, the family of the man James killed during last week's botched robbery attempt had pointed Cresha out of a photo lineup, identifying her as James' accomplice; which meant that she was now on the run for murder.

'I ain't goin' to no damn jail,' she thought to herself as she turned into the alley behind her Aunt Crystal's Laramie Avenue home.

She reversed into Crystal's garage and parked. She got out and closed the garage door, then walked around to the trunk with Treys on her left and Two-One on the right side of her. Grinding her teeth, she pressed a button on the Bentley's remote key, and the trunk popped open.

Cresha gasped as Kisha raised the AR-15 and squeezed the trigger.

Click. Click. Click. Click.

Kisha's mouth dropped open in shock. The assault rifle was empty.

The gunman that had forced her into the trunk swung a pistol at her face, knocking her out cold.

When she came to, she was being duct-taped to a chair in what looked like somebody's basement. Her left eye was completely swollen shut. Blood was skating down the side of her face.

Standing in front of her was Lacresha Radcliff. Cresha uncrossed her arms and put her hands on her hips.

"Bitch you gon' do me like this?" Kisha asked, in shock.

"Don't take it personal. My brother is dead because of your punk ass boyfriend. Now all I want is the money he took from Mone." Cresha dug in her purse and pulled out a flip phone. "What's his number?"

"I don't know."

"Don't fuckin' play wit' me, Kisha. I'll slit your throat as quick as I sliced up Deshell at the club that night. Try me if you want to."

Kisha shuddered as she envisioned a knife cutting through her neck. She kept her eye on Cresha. "I'm not lying, Cre. I don't remember his number. It's programmed into my—"

One of the dread-headed gunmen slapped Kisha across the face before she could finish her sentence.

"Let her talk, you dumbass!" Cresha snapped.

Kisha tasted blood. "I left my phone at home. His number is in my phone," she said.

"Well," Cresha said, flipping open the cheap camera phone, "what's your number then?"

Chapter 28

Kisha's phone was ringing when we walked through the door. I snatched it up and answered it.

"Who is this?"

"If I'm not mistaken, I'm the girl you pushed into Mone's bedroom before you and your friend blew his brains out. Remember that?"

I cast a brief glance at the phone screen and saw the name Lacresha, then clicked into the text messages and found a picture of Kisha posing in front of a stripper pole at Arnie's with a group of chicks. One of the girl's in the picture with her was the girl from Mone's stash house.

"Where is my girlfriend?"

"She's right here. Bitch got a black eye and a busted lip, but other than that she's fine. Give me the money you took from Mone and I'll let her go."

"Deal. I got it ready for you now. All I got left is, like, fifty racks, and you can have all of it. Just let her go."

"You're lying to me, Michael Love. I saw what was in that duffle bag. Lie to me again and see if I don't shoot this bitch in the head."

Wait till I catch you! is what I wanted to say as I walked to the bedroom to get the money, but I kept my mouth shut. I had to get Kisha back first.

"Weren't there four duffle bags?" Cresha asked. "I'm going to round that off to two hundred thousand, and I don't want a dollar less."

"Let me talk to Kisha," I said, dragging a duffle bag from under the bed.

Seconds later, Kisha's sobbing voice filled my ear and traveled straight down to my heart. I sat on the bed and let a long, heartfelt sigh escape me. Scrilla Man and Tyrone joined me on the bed.

"I'm… I'm okay," Kisha said. "Please, just give them the money. Give it to them so I can come home. *Please*, Mikey, I don't wanna die."

"I will, baby. Stay calm. I'ma take care of this."

"Of course you will," Lacresha cut in. "We'll meet on the front steps of John Hay Public School at midnight; 1025 North Laramie Avenue. Oh, and bring the boy that killed my brother with you."

She hung up and I turned to Tyrone. "I heard her," he said.

We sat in silence for a moment until Joe-Joe and Shay shouted for us to turn to the ABC 7 News. I cut on the TV and flipped to the channel.

Breaking News:
"Chicago Police are advising the public to be on the lookout for this African-American woman, Lacresha Radcliff. She's allegedly responsible for the murder of 40-year-old Michael Love Sr., who was killed last week inside his home in the 1300 block of South Troy Street. Police say the second man that was killed there is Suspect Radcliff's brother…"

I gazed at the photo of Lacresha Radcliff with my teeth clenched tightly. Until now, I had never in my life wanted to harm a woman; especially not a black woman. I *love* black women.bBut Lacresha?

"That bitch gotta go," I murmured coldly.

Chapter 29

I gave Tyrone the keys to the Expedition and sent him and Joe-Joe out to drop a quarter pound of Kush off to my nigga Chubb. The remaining four of us sat at the kitchen table passing around blunts of Kush and shooting ideas back and forth while they helped me count out the $200,000.

"I ain't know you had this much money," Scrilla Man said.

"Fuck this money," I replied through a cloud of smoke. "This money got Pops killed, got my nigga shot, and now it just got my girl kidnapped. I was better off without this shit."

Rose shook his head from left to right. "You can't let that bitch get away wit' all this bread, fam. We can park down the street somewhere, catch her leavin' and bang her whip up wit' them choppas."

"I just gotta get Kisha first. It's whatever after that." I pushed a $20,000 stack of hundreds to the side and kept counting.

The doorbell rang ten minutes later. I picked up my Glock 33 and Rose followed me to the front and down the stairs. I put my eye to the peephole, then hid the pistol under my shirt and opened the door.

It was Lil Cholly, the TVL who owned the custom detailing shop where I had taken my father's old Chevy. Lil Cholly was a big timer in the hood, and everybody knew it. He'd been moving kilos for years.

"Sorry to hear about Big Mike. My niggas at the shop fixed you up nice, though. Real nice," Lil Cholly said, stepping aside so I could see the car.

Parked behind Lil Cholly's pearl-white Panamera, my father's four-door Caprice was so stunning that I momentarily forgot all about my kidnapped girlfriend.

It was painted a dark, candy orange, and the thirty-inch rims that had it sitting so high above the ground, were the exact same color. A picture that me and Pops had taken at a family reunion before he went to prison was painted on the trunk. The passenger's side doors were open, exposing the orange leather interior.

I grabbed the keys from Lil Cholly and headed down the stairs with him, skimming my eyes around the street, watching my surroundings.

Several cars were driving by slowly; their passengers were eyeing the Caprice and shouting compliments.

"Yeah, this muhfucka cold, bruh," I said, walking around the car to admire it further. "On King James, this muhfucka serious."

Lil Cholly showed me how to open and close the stash-box. He also showed me the 15-inch speakers in the trunk, and the twelve TVs that had been installed inside the box Chevy. I was truly amazed. Now I had the flyest whip in the hood.

"Ay, lil fam," Rose shouted from the porch. He was watching a brown Buick that was racing down Millard toward me.

I moved out of the way just as it came to a screeching halt beside my brother's Escalade, which was parked behind the Caprice. Manny pushed open the driver's door and hopped out holding a wooden baseball bat. His face was swollen and bloodied from the beating he'd taken at the funeral.

"You niggas wanna fight now?!" he shouted, approaching me with the bat cocked back.

I did not hesitate.

I drew the Glock and quickly shot him four times in the chest. Then I stood over his grounded body and emptied the clip in his face.

"Police-ass nigga," I said, glowering down at his exploded head.

Without a word, Lil Cholly snatched the gun out of my hand, got in his Porsche, and sped off.

I turned and ran to the porch, glancing at the dozen or so shocked eyewitnesses that were running away from the murder scene. I wasn't worried about them snitching; from the infants to the elderly, everyone knew better than to go against the mob.

Chapter 30

Sitting beside his wife, Aesha Jenner, in the back seat of his matte black S600 Benz, King Royce was focused on the Dodge pick-up that had just pulled into the driveway of a modest two-story home, a block ahead of him. There were fifty kilos of cocaine stashed in the back of the pick-up. He had two of his Latin King soldiers delivering the drugs to Sosa, a young Black Disciple who had recently gained fame as a ruthless Chicago rap artist.

They were in Bellwood, Illinois, a suburban area not far from the Windy City where King Royce had long ago risen from the slums to become the multi-millionaire birdman that he was now. His wife was also wealthy, though she had earned her millions as the lead shoe designer at Prada, while his had come from getting kilos of cocaine and heroin from Mexico's reigning Costilla Cartel and selling them to gang leaders all across Chicago.

He donned a dull gray Tom Ford business suit; his wife, a form- fitting red Prada dress and matching five-inch heels. She was handling some business on her iPad and he was biting down on an unlit Cuban cigar, his stern eyes hidden behind the dark lenses of his expensive sunglasses.

"You need to hurry up and get our car back from that girl before the police get to her," Aesha said, her attention never shifting from the iPad. "I don't know why you're taking care of her in the first place. You're always trying to save those hoodrats. Leave them in the ghetto where they belong."

"I can't just leave *her* out there like that. She knows too much."

"And that doesn't bother you? What do you think she's going to tell the prosecutor to get her sentence reduced?"

"She won't say anything. We've already hired Britney Bostic, one of the cartel's lawyers. Cresha will more than likely beat the case. Even if she doesn't, she'll only serve a year or two."

Aesha shook her head. "No more strip clubs for you."

King Royce ignored his wife's last comment. He knew that he couldn't tell her the truth about why he was looking after Lacresha. He couldn't tell anyone, not even Lacresha herself.

He leaned forward in his seat as several young black men with dreads exited Sosa's home carrying duffle bags. He was paying the Costilla Cartel $10,000 per kilo and charging Sosa $17,000, which amounted to $350,000 in profit for this drug transaction.

His iPhone started ringing with a call from Lil Cholly, a Vice Lord he'd been dumping kilos on for the past few months. He eased back in his seat and answered. "Back at me already?"

"Nah," Lil Cholly said. "Shit gettin' too hot out this way. *Way too hot.* It's like the Wild West out here. Lil niggas shootin' everybody, police everywhere you look. Fuck this shit, I'm about to fly out to Florida for the rest of the summer, or at least till all this gunplay slow down a lil bit."

King Royce was silent as he pondered over all the money he would undoubtedly miss out on if Lil Cholly suddenly skipped town.

Then Lil Cholly offered a remedy to that monetary problem, and King Royce smiled tightly as he ended the call.

Seconds later, King Royce's driver turned the Benz around and, followed by two SUVs full of heavily armed Latin Kings, headed back to Chicago.

Chapter 31

An hour had passed since I'd blown Manny's brains out and I was more paranoid than ever. The Kush I'd smoked intensified my paranoia tenfold.

"There's about a hundred police out there," Shay said, peeking out the living room window.

I was pacing a tight circle in front of the wall-mounted flat-screen television. I was afraid that at any moment the CPD would come crashing through the door with their guns drawn; which is why I was holding my 9mm Glock with the 50-round drum in an unrelenting grip while I chewed the thumbnail of my other hand down to the flesh. I was determined to join Pops in the grave before I joined my niggas in prison.

My two Louis Vuitton duffle bags were on the floor next to the sofa. The $200,000 ransom was packed into one of them and the rest of my cash and drugs—aside from the $8000 I had in my pants pockets—was packed up in the other one.

"Nigga stop pacin'. You makin' me nervous," Scrilla Man said. He and Rose were standing near the door looking more paranoid than I was.

"They're letting people move their cars now," Shay said.

Thinking quickly, I put my pistol in one of the duffle bags, then picked both of them up and walked over to Shay.

"Here," I said, handing her the keys to the Caprice. "Put these bags in the trunk of that orange Chevy, drive down sixteenth to Trumbull, and park right there at the corner. We'll meet you there in five minutes."

"Nah, she gotta take my truck, bruh," Scrilla Man said. "We got two bricks in that muhfucka."

He was right. It was best to get all the drugs away from us as soon as possible. Scrilla Man gave Shay his keys and I took mine back.

"You niggas better not get me locked up," Shay said. She lifted the duffle bags and walked to the door. "Hand me my purse."

"Don't go out there lookin' all suspicious and shit," I advised.

Rose grabbed Shay's Chanel bag off the coffee table and gave it to her. I held my breath as she descended the staircase.

My heart dropped when Scrilla Man peeked out the window and murmured, "Damn! Shit, bruh!"

"What?!" I said.

"Cop just stopped her." I slapped my palms to my forehead. "She just put the bags down."

'Oh, shit!' was all that came to my mind.

"She diggin' through her purse for somethin' now. Prob'ly her ID." I held my breath again. "Aw, she good. She getting' in my truck now," Scrilla Man added a moment later.

We all let out a sigh of relief. We waited ten minutes before leaving out. Several police officers approached us as soon as we stepped off the porch. They asked for our IDs. I showed my driver's license, since my state ID was in Lacresha Radcliff's possession. They asked me if we had seen anything. Of course, we hadn't.

As I was getting behind the wheel of my Caprice, I glanced at the white sheet that covered the dead snitch's body and fought back the urge to smile. Then I started the engine, drove slowly to the corner, and released another sigh of relief as I made a right onto 16th Street.

Rose was the first to start laughing from the backseat. Scrilla Man followed suit, and soon I was laughing, too.

"Maaaan," Rose said, clapping his hands against the back of my seat, "I can't believe this shit. On Larry, lil fam, you's a certified nutcase."

"This the craziest day ever," Scrilla Man said, still laughing.

But our laughter diminished instantly when we made it to the corner of 16th and Trumbull.

My brother's Escalade was nowhere in sight.

***

Once again I found myself driving aimlessly through my neighborhood searching for a vehicle. A bunch of people had seen the Escalade driving down 16th—an SUV on thirty-inch rims was hard to miss—but no one had seen it make any stops. Furthermore, Shay wasn't answering our phone calls. For a while her phone just rang, and rang, and rang. Then it started going straight to voicemail.

"That bitch got us, lil bruh." Scrilla Man was shaking his head, texting Shay for the ninth time. "Bitch got our guns, our dope."

"Fam, that whole brick wasn't even mine," Rose said. He, too, was shaking his head. "I owe my Folks half o' dat."

"She can't get too far. I've been to her house before, wit' Kisha," I mumbled, hopefully. "Shit, but we ain't even strapped up. I left my choppa in the Expedition. Ain't no tellin' where Tyrone and Joe-Joe at."

I dialed Tyrone's number and got his voice mail.

'This really is the craziest day ever,' I thought, eyeing the gas meter as I prepared to hit the highway.

Shay lived in Michigan City, Indiana. I was on my way to pay her a visit.

Chapter 32

It only took Shay fifty minutes to make it to her small, one bedroom apartment in Michigan City, Indiana.

There were a few drug dealers and thugs living in Coolspring Apartments. But for the most part the complex of apartment buildings housed blacks, whites, and Hispanics who worked nine-to-fives and spent their spare time drinking, popping Molly's and x-pills, smoking weed and/or crack, and cheating on the lovers they claimed to be so faithful to. Michigan City was nothing like Chicago—the locals were more into fighting than shooting—but it was still a crazy little city, full of dope boys, easy girls, and all-out drama.

Shay pulled the Escalade into a parking space next to her boyfriend Berry's green Delta 88. Berry—an unknown Vice Lord from off Washington and Kostner on the west side of Chicago—was sitting in the Oldsmobile smoking weed with his right-hand man, Santana—a BD who was also from Chicago. The two of them looked visibly surprised to see Shay climbing out of an Escalade on thirties, and Shay was glad to see that their pistols were on their laps.

"Baby, we gotta hurry up and pack up so we can leave," Shay said, opening the Escalade's rear driver's side door to grab the duffle bags.

Berry stepped out of his car and flicked his blunt roach at the glass door of Shay's apartment building. He was light-skinned, shaped like a body-builder, and laughing like he always did when he smoked.

"Daaamn," he said, studying the Escalade's gaudy exterior. "Who you fuckin'? I see I'ma have to put a end to yo' lil Chicago trips. Last week you came home wearin' Louboutins, and this week you show up in a 'Lac truck, pullin' out Louis Vuitton duffle bags."

"Don't stop her now," Santana said as he got out and walked around the car. He was short and dark, with ridiculously long arms and a receding hairline that was worse than Lebron's.

"Nigga, like I told you before," Shay said, dropping the bags onto the ground and unzipping them, "let me do what I do best."

Berry and Santana immediately got excited. Shay smiled at her man as he dug his eager brown hands into one of the bags and pulled out a bundle of hundred dollar bills and Mikey's gun with the big drum magazine.

She slapped the cash and pistol out of his hands and laughed as they plummeted back into the duffle.

"Baby, we gotta pack up some stuff and leave here ASAP. The nigga I took this from has been here before and I just watched him kill a nigga in broad daylight."

"Fuck we need to pack for?" Berry asked. "We can go shoppin' wit' all this money."

"Boy, I ain't goin' nowhere without my shoes," Shay said as she picked up the duffle bags and rushed into her apartment.

Chapter 33

I stopped at a Speedway gas station when we made it into Michigan City, Indiana to fill up my gas tank. I ended up paying a middle-aged black couple a hundred dollars to lead me to Coolspring Apartments. The couple led us to the apartment complex's front entrance and I parked there as they drove away.

"What the fuck we gon' do now?" Scrilla Man asked. "We ain't got no guns. What if she got some niggas wit' her that's strapped up?"

"We gon' have to find out the hard way," I said.

Slowly, I cruised into the apartment complex, scanning my eyes around at the cars and people that were coming and going.

A dusty van full of hoodrats pulled up beside my Caprice. Its diver—an acne-faced dark-skinned girl with a tight little ponytail hanging out the back of her Bull's cap—stuck her head out the window and shouted, "Heeeey boy, where you from?" She was practically drooling over my rims.

"Flint, Michigan," I lied. "I'm out here lookin' for my cousin Shay."

"Who, skinny Shay?"

"Yeah."

The girl pointed toward the rear of the complex. "That's them leaving right there in that green Delta. That Escalade must be yours, too, huh?"

Ignoring the girl's question, I stepped on the gas and lanced toward the green Oldsmobile that was leaving out the complex's rear entrance.

Out of the corner of my eye, I saw Scrilla Man's SUV parked in front of Shay's apartment building. I hoped that I wasn't on a wild goose chase going after the Oldsmobile.

I wasn't.

Turning onto the deserted back road, I saw through the car's rear window that Shay was sitting in the backseat behind two men. Shay glanced over her shoulder and her eyes went buck as she caught sight of my rapidly approaching Caprice.

"Hold on, y'all," I said and rammed the back of the Oldsmobile. I wasn't prepared for what happened next.

The man in the Delta 88's passenger seat stuck a pistol out his window and started blasting, sending bullet after bullet through my windshield.

We all ducked down in the Chevy and I sped forward and rammed the Oldsmobile again.

The sound of gunfire ceased, replaced by the screeching of tires, and then the ear-piercing sound of crushing metal and shattering glass.

I stomped on the brake and cautiously raised my head.

The Oldsmobile was flipping sideways down the long, tree-lined road. It landed on its roof, with its tires spinning freely in the air.

The three of us got out and ran up to the upside-down wreckage.

Surprisingly, Shay and the other two passengers were still breathing, though just barely.

They would not be breathing for long.

I reached in the back window and grabbed my duffle bags, while Scrilla Man dragged Shay out the other side and demanded she tell him where the keys to his Escalade were.

After finding my Glock inside one of the duffle bags, I tossed the bags to Rose and walked around to where Scrilla

Man stood over Shay just as the nigga in the passenger's seat was attempting to crawl out of the car.

I aimed the Glock at his head and pulled the trigger, blowing his brains out. Then I squatted, reached into the car, and put two bullets in the side of the driver's head.

"I'm...sorry," Shay muttered, lying flat on the ground with a puddle of blood in her mouth. "I'm sorry, Mikey. Please..."

"Sorry ain't gon' cut it," I said icily. Then I put a bullet through her right eye.

Chapter 34

"Do you have any idea how hard it is to take care of a special needs baby all by yourself? Huh, Kisha? I have a daughter, who will *never* be able to see, and she doesn't even have a father. *I* don't even know who he is! I thought I was a damn virgin when I found out I was pregnant with my baby. I started dancing at Arnie's so I could pay my way through college and the next thing I knew, I was three weeks pregnant."

Kisha was sitting quietly in the chair with tears in her eyes and tape on her lips, listening to Lacresha's sad story. The two gunmen were fast asleep on the tattered sofa in the corner underneath the staircase. A Jill Scott album was blaring from somewhere upstairs and Kisha wondered if whoever was up there vibing to the music was aware of what was going on right under their feet.

"I think one of those nothin' ass hoes at the club slipped somethin' in my drink the night I got pregnant," Lacresha continued. "I remember having to do a bachelor's party with Platinum and Kitten around the time I got knocked up. But I don't even remember goin', let alone what went down when I got there." She wiped her moist eyes, shifted uncomfortably in the chair she was sitting in, and let out a short laugh. "I know this shit probably sound like somethin' out of *Player's Club*, but bitch I swear it's true."

There was a bottle of Remy Martin and a glass full of ice on the floor next to Cresha's chair. She and the gunmen had been drinking for most of the evening, and now the bottle was nearly empty. She leaned over and poured the last of the Remy into the glass. Kisha glanced at the clock on the wall and saw that it was 9:41 p.m.

'Two more hours and nineteen more minutes,' Kisha thought to herself. *'Lord, please let Mikey be there with that money.'*

Lacresha's monotonous sob story continued for the next half hour. She told Kisha that she planned to use the ransom money to get silicone injections in her butt. Then she'd move to Miami and get rich dancing in strip clubs, maybe even modeling.

"All I need is a fat ass to get me a baller," Cresha said as her phone began ringing. She looked at it and added, "This King Royce callin' me now. He rich as fuck, but the nigga won't pay for my surgery no matter how many times I beg his fine ass. He say I'm already *beautiful.* Evidently I ain't too damn beautiful if I'm broke!" Cre stood up to answer the call and headed toward the stairs. "I gotta pee, bitch. Be back in a minute," she said.

'Bitch, I gotta pee too,' thought Kisha.

The sound of the basement door awakened one of the gunmen. He got up and stretched. Then he walked to the staircase and looked up at the door. Kisha cringed as his menacing brown eyes shifted to her.

She squeezed her eyes shut and dropped her head, praying he wasn't thinking what she thought he was thinking.

But indeed he was.

He held his gun to her neck as he untaped her from the chair, threatening to kill her if she tried to fight or run. Kisha wanted to live so she didn't resist as he snatched her up from the chair and pushed her face against the wall.

He lifted her dress, ripped her panties off, and entered her from behind. A pained groan rumbled in Kisha's throat. The boy's dick was huge. It felt like someone was fucking her with a beer bottle.

She closed her eyes and again she prayed.

Chapter 35

We made it back to Chicago without incident and laid low at my Uncle Mutulu's home on 13th and Sawyer until 11:30. The three of us sat in the guest room, smoking bunts and reminiscing on the good and bad times we'd shared with Pops. Treecy came in and kicked it with us, but she didn't say much. Momma and Mutulu stayed in the kitchen with a few other relatives, listening to oldies and drinking their Crown Royal.

I had finally gotten a call from Tyrone during the ride home from Indiana. He and Joe-Joe were chilling out front in the Expedition when we stepped out the front door.

I told Tyrone to stay a few car-lengths behind us, and to be ready to set it off with my AK-47 if anything went sour.

Then I got in my Caprice with Scrilla Man and Rose and traveled the dark west side streets until I made it to John Hay public school on Laramie Avenue.

I looked at the time on my dashboard and saw that it was exactly midnight, twelve o'clock on the dot.

I held the nine millimeter Glock in my hand and waited.

"Somebody gon' die tonight and it ain't gon' be me," I said, clenching my fingers around the Glock on my lap as the yellow Bentley coupe pulled up and parked across the street from my candy-orange box Chevy Caprice. A black S600 Benz and two black Suburbans pulled in behind the Bentley.

It was one minute after midnight on the twelfth of July and, except for the glossy-eyed gray cat that was sitting on the steps of John Hay Public School, Laramie Avenue was completely deserted.

My girlfriend, Kisha, had been kidnapped hours earlier, shortly after my father's funeral. I was sitting on the deserted street with the $200,000 ransom, waiting to get her back.

"Chill out, lil bruh," said Scrilla Man, my older brother. He was seated beside me and his maternal cousin, Rose, was in the backseat. They too had pistols on their laps, though their hands were not as tightly glued to their weapons as mine.

I had a good reason for my overly cautious demeanor. Over the past week, my father had been killed during a robbery attempt at our home, my lil guy Tyrone had been shot twice during the same incident; I had gotten my Monte Carlo shot up right before my father's funeral. I'd beaten up Manny—a nigga who'd set up my father in a drug sting—at the funeral; and when he showed up outside Kisha's house wielding a baseball bat, I shot him dead in the middle of the street. Then almost half of a million dollars in cash and drugs—basically everything I had—was stolen from me a couple of hours ago, and getting it back had nearly cost me my life.

I pushed open my door, swung my legs out, and hopped down to the curb; my Chevy's lift-kit and massive 30-inch rims had it sitting high above the ground.

To my surprise, Kisha and my nigga Lil Cholly stepped out of the Bentley just as I was grabbing my Louis Vuitton duffle bag from the seat next to Rose. Lil Cholly was one of the Traveling Vice Lords who had brought me into the mob when I was nine years old. He was one of Chicago's top-echelon drug pushers, and the car shop he owned had turned my Caprice into the dream car that it now was—well, minus the three fresh bullet holes in the windshield, and the dented front bumper, indelible reminders of the carnage I'd just left in Indiana.

I left the duffle in the backseat and prepared to empty my Glock's 50-round drum magazine as Kisha ran across the street and fell into my arms. I wondered why Lil Cholly was with her.

"Everything's good, lil bruh," Lil Cholly said. "My plug found out one of his lil hoes had kidnapped Kisha. We just went and got her 'bout twenty minutes ago."

"Kisha, get in the car, baby," I said, snatching open Rose's door.

He and Scrilla Man got out as Kisha got in. My heart ached at the sight of her badly swollen eye. Her usually pretty dark-brown face looked awkward all bloodied and beaten, and I was not happy about it.

From halfway down the block, Kisha's white Expedition came speeding toward us. It screeched to a stop behind my Chevy. Tyrone emerged from the driver's door, aiming my AK-47 at the Bentley. His younger cousin Joe-Joe hopped out with a chrome-plated .45 trained on one of the Suburbans.

"Y'all chill out!" Lil Cholly shouted.

Lil Cholly was a three-star Universal Elite for our branch of Vice Lords, so his word was gold. Tyrone and Joe-Joe lowered their weapons. But I was still ready for war.

"Where dat bitch at?" I snapped, scowling at the Bentley.

Dat bitch was Lacresha Radcliff, the woman responsible for my father's murder, and for Kisha's kidnapping.

"You might not ever see her again, lil bruh. She's wanted for murder—"

"Yeah, no shit."

"Royce just gave her a hundred thousand and sent her to Florida somewhere." Lil Cholly put a hand on my shoulder. "I know, bruh… she kidnapped your girl and had your old man killed. But ain't shit we can do about that now. Take Kisha and get out of town for a week or two. Leave all this bullshit in the rearview and focus on the road ahead. Shit, I'm about to leave for the rest of the summer. Too many bodies droppin' in the hood." He leaned close and whispered, "My plug gon' fuck with you from now on. I told him about you and he wanna do business with you while I'm gone. It's cartel business, though, so don't accept nothin' you can't move."

I didn't say a word. The woman responsible for my father's murder was getting away and I was not happy about it.

I turned and walked around to my driver's door, glowering across the street at the Bentley, and the Benz, and the two Suburbans.

"Just think it over, lil bruh," Lil Cholly said as I got in the car. "Call me next week and let me know what you wanna do."

Grinding my teeth together, I busted a U-turn and sped off toward Chicago Avenue, squeezing the handle of my Glock so tightly that my fingers went numb.

Chapter 36

Five Days Later…

"What are you reading?" Kisha asked sleepily as she sat up in bed and rested her cheek on my shoulder.

"A Gangster's Daughter, by Leo Sullivan," I said, keeping my eyes on the Kindle tablet cradled in my hands.

"Mikey, what time is it?"

I glanced at my most prized possession—a $40,000 rose-gold Rolex watch.

"Five o'clock… in other words, it's time for you to get up and fix me somethin' to eat, preferably some pancakes, scrambled eggs, beef sausages, and grits. Your eye done healed up now, so you ain't got no excuses. Get to it."

Her pretty lips curled up into an angelic smile. One of her hands began massaging my smoothly shaven brown scalp, while the other slipped beneath the covers and caressed my rock-hard six-pack. I felt her fingernails rake across the large VICE LORD tattoo that was arched across my abdomen. Her softly roaming palms set a fire in my loins, and my dick automatically stiffened.

"You should write a book," Kisha said, kissing my shoulder. "Name it *Gangster's Son*. Tell everybody about your daddy and how you were raised here in Chicago."

"I ain't writin' no book," I said as I laid the Kindle tablet on my bedside table. "I'm already a gangster's son. Fuck I need to write about it for?"

Kisha climbed on top of me and regarded me with her salacious smile. She palmed and kneaded my pectoral muscles, and my dick grew harder as her warm, naked pussy brushed across its throbbing underside. "My eye lookin' any better?" she asked.

"Yup," I said, not even looking at her eye, which was now only slightly bruised; I was ogling the taut brown nipples that were protruding from the dark areolas of her perky little breasts.

Snickering briefly, she slapped my chest. "Nigga, you ain't even lookin' at my face." She crawled backward, taking the covers with her, and grabbed my nine inch phallus with both hands.

I watched as she swirled her tongue around the crown of it before opening her mouth and sucking it in. It was then that I finally glimpsed her eye. There was only a thin black line under her lower eyelid, but her eye was still bloodshot. The minor bruising did not take away from her

chocolate beauty. Kisha was as beautiful as Gabrielle Union. In fact, she looked a lot like the dark-hued young girl from the movie *Bronx Tale*.

About a minute later, she turned around and lowered her wet, sweet-scented pussy down to my mouth, and I ate it like a hungry fat kid.

We were in the master bedroom of our new home: a two-bedroom condominium in the affluent Lincoln Park neighborhood. My uncle, Mutulu, owned the building so I hadn't gone through much to get the apartment. Kisha was already back to stripping at Arnie's—she claimed pole-dancing helped her forget about the rape she'd experienced at the hands of her kidnappers—and the $1,000 or so that she made every night she worked was more than enough to legitimately pay our bills. Plus, I still had over $400,000 in cash, three pounds of Kush, and eighteen ounces of cocaine, so money was not an issue. Uncle Mutulu's only stipulation was that I leave the streets alone for good.

I wasn't sure if I could.

Chapter 37

Ninety degrees of warm, sticky heat clung to the sweaty chocolate skin of two teenagers on the corner of 15th Street and Trumbull Avenue. They were seventeen year old Tyrone and his younger, darker cousin Joe-Joe.

Clad in Jordan sneakers, baggy Pelle Pelle jeans, and fresh white t- shits, the two boys were entertaining a group of four hood chicks while simultaneously watching the drug deals going down a block away on Homan. *SICKO MOBB* was airbrushed across the chests of Tyrone and Joe- Joe's white tees in brown and gold to match the Lois Vuitton bandanas that were hanging out of their left back pockets.

"Baby, can we go home now?" Jessica asked. She was a redbone dime-piece that had been Tyrone's girlfriend for the past two weeks or so. She was studying the 26-inch rims beneath the frame of Tyrone's red Monte Carlo. With her perfectly manicured fingertips tucked in the back pockets of the tight denim shorts that barely made it over the huge swells of her ass, she sucked her teeth and added, "Shit, Ty, it's eleven in the damn mornin' and we've been out here since eleven last night. I'm tired, hot, and hungover."

"We'll leave in a few minutes, as soon as my lil niggas get rid of that last jab." Tyrone flicked his eyes up and down 15th like he did every couple of minutes, making sure there were no CPD patrol cars or potential robbers creeping up on him and his team of dealers. His guys had already been robbed once that week. He'd lost $900 and a half ounce of crack in that incident, and he definitely wasn't about to take any more losses.

Adjusting the sling on his arm—he'd caught two bullets in the shoulder the previous week—Tyrone shifted his eyes back to Jessica. He hated having her around him all the time, but he knew better than to leave her alone with her slutty friends, all of whom had three or four kids by a plethora of drug dealers that were now either dead, in jail, or somewhere in bed with new hood-rats. Plus, Jessica had already cheated on him with Mikey, one of Ty's closest friends.

An ingratiating smile burgeoned on Tyrone's face as he noticed that the five younger Vice Lords on Homan were walking toward him. Two of them—Dave and Ceno—were his dealers, and the other three were armed security.

Tyrone got in his car with Ceno and rolled up the tinted windows. Ceno dug in his pockets and pulled out several rubber-banded knots of cash. He handed all but one of them to Tyrone.

"That's three bands, joe," Ceno said, thumbing through his own pile of cash. "We got another show at the Cadillac Theatre tonight; should be able to pop off at least three more ounces after that."

Tyrone nodded and concentrated on counting through the knots of drug money. Last night, he'd given Ceno three ounces of hard, and the three grand was his payment.

He had gotten the dope from Mikey on the day of Kisha's kidnapping. A kilo of soft, a pound of Kush, the Monte Carlo on twenty- sixes—all had been gifts presented to Tyrone for killing the man who'd killed Mikey's father.

The brick of coke had pushed Tyrone to the top of his block's crack-dealer's hierarchy. There were a few others making more cash than he was, but they were heroin dealers. With two twelve-hour shifts of young gangbangers pumping his work, Tyrone was clearing $7,000 per day, and he was loving every minute of it. He had cooked the thirty-six ounces of soft into forty-four ounces of hard. Now he was down twenty-four zips and up $24,000, which he hoped would grow to $28,000 by the end of his next shift of workers.

"You know that lame ass nigga Ton been ridin' around tellin' muhfuckas what he gon' do to Mikey n'em when he catch 'em," Ceno said. "Don't e'en trip though, we gon' catch Ton at the show tonight and stomp his ass out."

Tyrone shook his head as he slipped the $3,000 into his pocket. "Man, Ton big goofy ass ain't gon' do shit. You and Lil Trav need to be writin' new music. This Sicko Mobb shit ain't gon' last no time if y'all ain't consistent. Let me deal wit' Ton."

"Shit, he ain't nobody to deal with."

"Good, so we agree. I'll talk to him and see if I can squash that shit before he fuck around and get killed. Here." Tyrone opened his glove compartment, took out a white paper bag, and handed it to Ceno. "Lay that on the next shift when they get here. That's four zips. Tell Lil Trav I need forty-four hundred off this. Same goes for you tonight. Gotta make eleven off every zip from now until I go back to the store next week."

"Shit, I'm Gucci-ball wit' dat. We pullin' seventeen-fifty off every zip anyway. Got everybody eatin'."

"Ain't that what it's about?" Tyrone asked.

"Hell muhfuckin' yeah, nigga," Ceno said with a winning smile. "On King James, joe, we gon' be eatin' like Cup n'em used to eat when they had the hood sowed up. All you gotta do is keep the work comin' in. And let us throw in next time to grab at least a nine piece."

"I gotchoo." Tyrone reached over and shook up—the TVL handshake—with Ceno, and then turned on the CD player as Ceno got out and headed up the street with the other young Vice Lords.

Jessica took Ceno's place in the passenger's seat. She lowered the volume on Kanye West's *Yeezus* album. Tyrone eyed her luscious pink-glossed lips as she turned to him and sighed.

"Can we please go home now?" Jessica asked, leaning her seat forward to let Joe-Joe into the backseat.

Joe-Joe got in with his eyes glued to his phone, and Jessica shut the door. She crossed her arms over her chest, put her back against the door, and scowled at Tyrone until he chuckled and started the engine.

"Calm down, baby. We're leavin' now," Tyrone muttered, getting ready to drive off.

But before he could pull off, he heard something that made him freeze—the sharp screeching of tires a block behind him.

He looked back just in time to see the smoke-gray Jeep speeding up alongside his Chevy.

The Jeep stopped and a large black man with a terribly swollen face emerged from the driver's door with a chrome nine millimeter pistol in his mammoth brown hand.

It was Ton.

Chapter 38

"Mikey are you gonna take the trash out? It's stinkin' up the kitchen," Kisha shouted.

"Yeah, give me a minute. I'm on Facebook."

I was sitting on our white leather sofa, wearing a fresh pair of gray sweatpants over brand new Louis Vuitton sneakers and scrolling down my Facebook newsfeed on my new Samsung Galaxy smartphone. A few of my family members were posting about how much they missed my father. I "liked" those posts, along with a few pictures and other posts from some people I knew.

And then I saw her.

I clicked "like" on the picture as soon as I saw it. There were two girls in the picture, a pretty chocolate girl in a camouflaged military uniform and a short-haired redbone with the fattest ass I'd ever seen on Facebook. The photo had been uploaded by Candice Howard and the caption read, "My sis Kesa's home from Iraq!"

My mouth dropped open as I took in the beauty of the girls' faces, and just then Kisha entered the living room with her hands on the hips of her short, black dress and a petulant scowl on her sexy, brown face.

"Baby, can you *please* take out the garbage before my sisters get here from the airport? They'll be here any minute now. Facebook will still be there when you get back."

I looked across the room at her; my brows knitted quizzically together. "I don't remember you sayin' shit about no sisters comin' over."

"Boy, didn't I tell you the other day that Kesa was staying here with us when she get back from her tour in—"

"A'ight, Kisha," I said, getting up. "I'll take it out right now." I breezed past her and into the kitchen, lifted the jam-packed bag out of the trashcan, and made it to our front door in record time.

"You wait one gotdamn minute," Kisha said. She crossed her arms and squinted her eyes at me. "What the hell you movin' so fast for?"

I cracked a smile. To be honest, I didn't remember Kisha mentioning anything about her sisters coming to stay with us—I'd never even met her sisters—but I was always glad to have more women around.

"Take that big stupid ass grin off yo' face," Kisha snapped. "I know what the hell you're thinkin', and trust me, it ain't gon' happen. Kesa and Candice should only be here for a week or two. Keep yo' hands to yourself, or I'm puttin' mine on you."

The doorbell chimed at that very moment.

Still smiling, I opened the door and stepped out into the hallway.

Kesa and Candice were standing just outside the glass door at the bottom of the staircase. For a second I thought they were smiling and waving at me, until I looked back and saw Kisha tailing me down the stairs.

I pushed the door open and said, "Hey, how y'all doing?" Then I walked to the dumpster and disposed of the garbage, trying my best not to drool over the size of Candice's mammoth derriere.

My phone rang. It was my lil nigga Tyrone.

I headed toward the three sisters with the phone to my ear.

"Bruh," Tyrone said uneasily, "dat nigga Ton just hopped out and put a choppa in my face! Talkin' 'bout he lookin' for you."

I stopped in my tracks, gazing vacantly at Kisha as she and her sisters pulled five suitcases into our building.

Tyrone went on, "Nigga lucky I didn't have dat fo'fifth. Don't e'en trip, though. We out here strapped up now, sittin' right here in front of his bitch crib."

"I'm on my way out there now, bruh." I dug into my pocket for my car keys.

"Nah, stay at home," Tyrone suggested. "We got this. But what I do need you to do is holla at that nigga Lil Cholly to get us some more product. I'll be all out in a few days."

I used the remote to unlock the doors on my box Chevy, climbed in behind the wheel, and quickly started the engine.

"I still got a half thang for fifteen," I said. "Shit, let me get that."

"I gotchoo. 'Bout to come out there and chop that fuck nigga up first, though."

"Bruh, didn't I just tell you we got this? Lay da fuck back, nigga. You done put in enough work. I'ma slide through soon's we handle this nigga, joe. On King James."

Grinding my teeth together, I sighed and agreed to stay home. After ending the call, I pressed my forehead against the woodgrain steering wheel and closed my eyes. I'd done a lot of dirt over the past week, and now I was regretting jumping on Ton with my brother Scrilla Man and his cousin Rose. I had started the fight without reason, and now Ton wanted revenge.

I couldn't blame him, but he had me fucked up if he thought he was going to kill me.

A knock at my window snatched me away from my thoughts. I raised my head and saw Candice's beautiful, reddish-brown face glowering in at me with what seemed to be a sickened expression. Her eyes were squinted and the corner of her pink-painted lips was lifted.

"Hey, boy." She pulled my door open and my eyes immediately went to her small gray boy shorts, and then up to the three letters that stretched across the chest of her pink halter: *DEA*.

I frowned. "What? And why you got a *DEA* shirt on?"

"Don't worry about it." Candice stepped aside as I got out of the car.

"Man, what the fuck you want?" I asked, already grinning.

Candice reciprocated with a smile of her own. She grabbed her hips and looked me up and down. "Boy, what's yo name again?"

"Mikey."

"Mikey... hmmm... You look a'ight, I guess. I just wanted to come and get a good look at the nigga that's fuckin' my sister, make sure you ain't no lame. My family don't do lames."

"I'm a million miles from lame. My daddy didn't raise none o'dem."

"Hmmm... Well... nice to meet you." Candice reached out to shake my hand. "I'm Agent Candice Howard, Chicago DEA."

My heart dropped to my stomach.

Chapter 39

Ton didn't stand a chance.

When he pulled up and parked his girlfriend's Jeep in front of their home on the corner of 16th and Drake, Tyrone and Joe-Joe were standing outside the convenience store across the street. Their shirts were lifted in the back by the protruding thirty-round magazines of their Ruger pistols. They were mixed in among a crowd of Drake Street TVLs and Jessica was behind the wheel of Tyrone's Monte Carlo at the curb; she had her head down and her hands clasped together, praying.

As soon as Ton pushed open his driver's door, Tyrone and Joe-Joe drew their guns and opened fire, sending round after devastating round into Ton's body. They didn't stop shooting until he was slumped over on the passenger's seat with one bullet-riddled leg hanging out the open driver's door.

Everyone on the corner fled hastily, either on foot or in their cars. "Hurry up and get in!" Jessica shrieked, flicking her nervous, terrified eyes at every car that sped past.

Joe-Joe looked to Tyrone for his next move.

"Think he dead?" Tyrone asked his younger cousin.

"Nigga, let's go! Hell yeah he dead!" Joe-Joe grabbed a handful of Tyrone's shirt, ran to the Monte Carlo's passenger door, snatched it open, and pushed Tyrone in beside Jessica. Then he slipped into the backseat mere seconds before Jessica busted a U-turn and sped off down 16th Street.

Tyrone noticed that Jessica's hands were trembling on the steering wheel and her knees were knocking together incessantly. But he didn't care about her being upset. *That's what she get for fuckin' my nigga Mikey,'* he thought as he raised his phone and dialed Mikey's number.

"What up, joe?" Mikey answered.

"Shit. We just handled dat one situation. About to go lay down till later on. You can stick a fork in Ton, though," Tyrone chuckled. "His ass is cooked."

Chapter 40

"A'ight, lil bruh. Damn… tell Lil Trav n'em to shut down shop until shit die down a lil bit. And stay in the house until I get there later on."

Shaking my head, I put the phone down next to the LV duffle on my bed and sat down, no longer paying attention to the mound of cash in my closed fist, nor the duffle bag full of cash, guns, coke, and Kush. I had locked myself in the bedroom to think over a few things—the situation with Ton, Lil Cholly's promise to plug me with his drug connect—and to get away from Kisha's police ass sister.

Now, all I could think about was the fight I'd started with Ton last week, and what it had led to today. I wondered if Ton was dead like my father and the many others that had been murdered over the past week.

'I gotta get outta dis shit,' I thought as the wriggling sound of the doorknob jarred me from my reverie.

"Boy, open up the door," Kisha said.

Reluctantly, I got up and unlocked the door. I was already back on the bed when Kisha sauntered in and shut the door behind her.

"Lock it," I said.

"Why?"

"Fuck you mean 'why'? 'Cause yo' sister the DEA!"

"Who, Candice?" A sugary smirk lit up Kisha's face as she crossed the room and mounted my lap. "Mikey, my sister is not employed with the DEA. Her and Kesa's dad is a DEA agent and Kesa's about to be a Chicago police officer. But Candice ain't no damn DEA. That bitch don't do nothin' but fuck and suck them dope boys for their money."

"Kinda like you do me," I said, falling back on one elbow.

"Negro, please. That's *our* money." She eased forward and moved her face so close to mine that our noses touched. "Speaking of which"—she snatched the pile of hundred-dollar bills out of my hand—"I need like thirty-eight hundred... just until next week."

I looked at her like she was crazy.

"*Babyyyyyy*," Kisha whined. She grabbed my ears and kissed my lips. "I told you I wanted those new Louboutins and a Chanel bag. And I gotta get my hair and nails redone for the concert tonight."

"Fuck that got to do wit' me?" I thumbed her dress up to her narrow waist and cradled her ass in my palms, watching as she counted out the bills on my shirt. "Ain't you supposed to be going to Shay's funeral today?"

Kisha shrugged, "Candice and Kesa are here now. Can't leave them here while I'm way out there in Indiana."

She got up and walked to the dresser to put the $3,800 in her Coach bag. I stuffed the remaining $6,200 in my pocket while gazing at her ample backside. My dick was throbbing in my pants when she returned to the bed. I quickly pushed her onto her back and got on top of her.

"You gon' quit spendin' all my muhfuckin' money. That shit don't grow on trees." I kissed her smiling lips, and then slipped a hand in her panties and assaulted her clit with my fingertips.

"Well," Kisha said and let out an involuntary moan. "I'm wifey. I deserve everything I get from yo' bald-headed ass. Mmmm... Why do you always *do* that?" She bit my lower lip and dug her impeccably manicured and painted fingertips into my back.

"Shut up." Already overwhelmingly hungry for her juices, I moved down between her smooth dark thighs and eyed the wet feast that awaited me.

As always, I dipped my tongue in her warm, tasty center, and then initiated a tongue fight with her palpitating clitoris. I felt her hands squeezing and rubbing my bald scalp. The scent of her sweet womanhood was more delectable than a Thanksgiving dinner.

I knew she was on the brink of climaxing when she clamped my head in her hands and started winding her hips ecstatically. I sealed my lips around her clit and licked it until she stiffened and vice-gripped my head between her soft thighs.

I lapped up her escaping juices as I pulled off my shirt and dropped my sweatpants.

"Mmm, I love you so much," Kisha said, pulling me down for a kiss.

She gasped and stabbed her fingernails in my back as I plunged deeply into her juicy pussy. I kissed her gaping mouth and started fucking her like I always did—ruthlessly, pounding all the way in with every thrust.

"You love me?" I asked.

"I love you," she said.

"You love me? That what you said?" "Yes, Mikey. Yes, Mikey. Yesssssss!"

I grinned widely. Leaning back, I gazed down at my glistening wet pole as I slammed in and out of her. The sweet scent of her Beyoncé perfume and the palatable aroma of her sex wafted up to my nostrils and sent me into overdrive. I turned her over and continued giving her the thug passion she was always so eager to get.

Suddenly, the bedroom door creaked open. I looked back and saw Kesa and Candice standing in the doorway with their hands planted on their hips. They wore ear-to-ear smiles, and Candice was licking her lips.

"Daaamn, nigga," Candice said, stepping around to the side of the bed for a better view. "That's how you do my sister?" She sounded excited.

"Mmm... girl it's... gooood, too," Kisha muttered between gasps and moans.

Kesa sucked her teeth and turned to leave. I squeezed Kisha's waist as my scrotum tightened and emptied.

Spent, I fell over to the side of her, studying her elated expression.

"Boy, you can't keep beatin' my shit up like that. Pretty soon I ain't gon' have no damn walls," Kisha said, getting up. She took some wet wipes out of her purse and wiped the dripping semen from her pussy. "I'm about to take Kesa shopping for a few things. You headin' out west?" She tossed me a wet wipe.

"On my way out there now," I said and caught Candice staring at my flaccid muscle as I cleaned it and pulled up my boxers and sweatpants. I didn't say anything about it; Kisha did.

"Bitch, what is you lookin' at? Fix yo' eyes 'for I fuck around and fix 'em for you. Michael Love is all mines, and I'll fuck up *everybody* about mine."

Candice sucked her teeth and crossed her arms. "Ain't nobody lookin' at this nigga."

"Good." Kisha picked up her Coach bag and turned to me. "Can you do me a favor and drop this hoe off on Chicago Avenue and Lawndale? We're going out tonight and she forgot to bring her outfit."

"I gotchoo," I said, and grabbed my duffle.

We got our things together and left the apartment a minute later.

I contemplated calling Lil Cholly to get some more dope as I jogged down the stairs ahead of the girls. But first I had to make sure my young niggas were safe from Ton's family, particularly his two cousins—Yellow, a short, light-skinned goon from the Low End, and Black Cory, an equally violent CVL from East Chicago. I knew that they were probably on their way to my neighborhood with trunks full of assault rifles. Word on the street was that Yellow had murdered over forty niggas on the south side, not including the many innocent bystanders that were wounded and sometimes killed during those shootings. And Black Cory—a coal-black gunslinger with a mouth full of gold teeth—was just as ruthless.

Emerging from the building, I paused and took in the diverse faces of my new neighbors, whites, Asians, and Hispanics that had never spent a single moment in Chicago's perilous black ghettos.

"Are those thirties?" Candice asked as we walked to my box Chevy.

"Yup."

"How much you pay for 'em?" "Enough."

Candice sucked her teeth and headed around to the passenger's side. I found myself staring wantonly at her incredibly thick derriere. Her ass was like Mars times two in those tight little shorts, and her bow-legged walk made her too irresistible to look away from.

I should have been looking elsewhere.

Just as Kisha was pulling off in her white Expedition, a tan- colored Buick came speeding down the street toward me. Candice jumped out of the way just in time to avoid getting hit and the Buick screeched to a stop next to my car.

I immediately recognized the two dread-headed teens that leapt out with twin AK-47s aimed in my direction. They were the same boys who'd kidnapped Kisha last week, the same boys who'd tried to kill me last week. I knew from Kisha that their nicknames were Two-One and Treys.

"Hahaaaa!" said the darker of the two as they moved closer.

"We caught you with that sack, didn't we? Nigga, run me dat duffle 'fore I go nuts out here."

My heart started pounding. Adrenaline surged. Angrily grinding my teeth together, I threw him the duffle bag and turned to glower at the dark brown woman in the Buick's driver's seat. It was Lacresha Radcliff, and she was glowering right back at me.

"Bitch ass nigga, I should have 'em kill yo' ass like my brotha killed yo' weak ass daddy." Cresha got out of the car and the goon handed her the duffle. Impervious to the frantically running pedestrians, she opened the duffle bag, glanced in, and smiled. "I'll let you slide this time. But tell your little friend—the one that killed my brother—that his ass is dead. Oh, and thanks for the money. We needed it."

I was livid. The two gunmen kept their sights on me as they all got in the rusty old Park Avenue. Lacresha rolled down the driver's window and shouted, "By the way... nice car. I like the burnt orange paint and the matchin' thirties. You'll look good pullin' up at Taco Bell to fill out that application later."

She dropped her head back and laughed. I had no choice but to stand there and watch her speed off with all of my cash and dope. Foolishly, I had stashed my handguns inside the duffle instead of keeping them on my waist where they belonged.

"Oh my God," Candice murmured, holding her hands to her mouth. "I thought they was gon' kill us."

"Get in the car." I snatched open my door and got in, wondering how Lacresha had found me.

Chapter 41

With Twista's *Adrenaline Rush* hammering out of the six 12" speakers in my trunk, I stomped on the gas pedal and my burnt orange Caprice launched forward, suspended over the other cars by its matching set of 30" rims. The dozen or so shock-stricken onlookers were all on their phones, presumably with 911; I wasn't hanging around for that.

"Nigga, if you don't slow down!" Candice shrieked. She put on her seatbelt and then clamped her hands onto the dashboard as I veered around a black Mercedes on North Lincoln Park West. "You are driving through a rich ass area that is literally *full* of white folks. Slow the fuck down before we get pulled over."

Reluctantly, I slowed the Chevy and lifted my phone to call Kisha—mainly to let her know that I'd just been robbed, and also to get my $3,000 back. But an incoming call from Lil Cholly came in before I could reach Kisha's number.

He didn't get a word out.

"Nigga," I snapped, "tell that bitch Lacresha *and* that fuck connect, if I don't get that duffle back wit' *everything* in it, me and my lil niggas gon'—"

"Wait, wait, wait, lil homie," Lil Cholly interrupted. "What the fuck are you talkin' about?"

I took an already rolled blunt of Kush out of my ashtray and lit it as I told him about the robbery. I checked my side and rearview mirrors, searching for the Buick, and then reached under my leather seat and grabbed the cold steel of what was now my only means of defense until I got to the hood—a chrome-plated nine millimeter Ruger. I had found it in my father's closet a few days ago, and now I was happy I had.

When I was done speaking, Lil Cholly paused for a moment, then he said, "Damn... she was in the room wit' us when that stripper got your address from Kisha. Deshell had Kisha on speakerphone when we got the address, and Cre was sittin' right next to her. *Damn.* I wasn't thinkin'. Shit, I was too focused on gettin' the deal set up for you. Look bruh; don't even worry about that loss. I'm two cars behind you in the black S600. Drive to the Louis Vuitton store on Michigan Avenue."

I ended the call abruptly, dropped the phone onto my lap, and squeezed the steering wheel with both hands as I clenched my teeth and glanced at the clean black Mercedes in my rearview mirror.

Chapter 42

"Pull over in front of the yellow house and leave this raggedy mothafucka running," Lacresha muttered coldly.

She and her two young goons—Two-One and Treys—were in the backseat of Kisha's SUV; the boys were holding their assault rifles and

flicking their eyes at every passing car on Laramie, while Lacresha counted through the bundles of cash in Mikey's duffle bag.

"Hurry up and give me my cut," Kisha said, nervously biting a thumbnail as she pulled over and parked. Her sister, Kesa, was turned sideways in the passenger's seat with the barrel of a Glock pressed against the back of her seat, ready to blast a hole through the young goons if they tried anything funny.

A few minutes later, Cre handed Kisha several rubber-banded piles of twenties, fifties and hundreds. Kisha counted the money, and then pushed it all down inside her large Coach bag. A sigh of relief blew from her lips as she watched the gunmen slip their long weapons down their pant legs and exit the rear passenger's side door with Cre.

"How much did you get?" Kesa asked as Kisha sped away from the curb.

"A hundred thousand," Kisha said, already back to chewing her thumb nail. "Mikey will kill me if he ever finds out about this." She sucked in a deep breath and made a left onto Chicago Avenue. "I'm giving you and Candice ten thousand apiece."

Kesa dropped the Glock in her purse and pulled out her shiny new Chicago Police Department badge. She'd passed the academy's final exam shortly before being deployed to Iraq nine months ago, and her first full day as a CPD officer was only four days away.

"Hope Candice can keep her mouth shut," Kisha mumbled.

"Come on now, sis. We've done this a hundred times before. Trust me, she won't say a thing. All we have to do is make sure *you* don't slip up and tell Mikey." Kesa shook her head. "Why'd you set him up anyway? I thought he was your man."

"Bitch, that nigga got me kidnapped and raped last week, and it was all because of that four hundred thousand dollars. That nigga ain't even gave me ten grand. He owed me this money."

Just then, Kisha's phone rang with a call from Mikey. "That's him right there, ain't it?" asked Kesa.

Kisha nodded yes and, after a brief moment of contemplation, she answered the call.

"You know it's over, right?"

"What?"

"You heard what the fuck I said. You tellin' niggas where I lay my head. Look, pack up everything you got and get the fuck out *today*!" I dropped my phone and threw my back against the seat, gritting my teeth and holding my gun in a tight grip. I was parked curbside in front of the Louis Vuitton store and the black Mercedes was pulling up behind me.

"Did you just put my sister out?" Candice asked.

"Yup. And I'm puttin' you out, too. Get the fuck out my car."

"Why you tryna put me out? I ain't did nothin' to you." She crossed her arms over her chest and glared at me. Then she said, "You know what? Fuck you. Hope they rob yo' ass again." She pushed open her door, stepped out, and slammed it shut.

I gazed lustfully at her huge ass as she stomped away. She made it about halfway down the block before some guy in a silver BMW convertible pulled over and scooped her up.

Lil Cholly got out of the Benz and took Candice's place in the seat next to me.

"Maaan, bruh," he said, "who the hell was *that*? *Damn*, she thick!"

I gritted my teeth and kept quiet. A part of me was wondering why Lil Cholly was still hanging around the woman whose brother had killed my father; the woman who'd had Kisha kidnapped and raped; the woman who had just gotten away with my brand new Louis Vuitton duffle bag and all the cash and drugs it contained.

My fingers tightened around the pistol.

Noticing the gun, Cholly said, "Chill out, lil bruh. Trust me, Royce didn't have nothin' to do with that shit. If he did, he wouldn't have twenty-five bricks waitin' on you outside your crib right now. Bruh, he's plugged with a Mexican drug cartel. Whatever you had in that duffle bag ain't nothin' to him, so don't even trip about it. He gon' check that bitch and get everything they took right back to you, and all he want is twelve bands off every brick. You can sell them bitches for thirty apiece if you want to, get all the way back."

"Just make sure he get my bread from that bitch, or I'm at his head, too. And tell him to give me her address. I'm payin' her a visit."

"He ain't givin' up Lacresha's address to nobody. I already tried gettin' it twice for you. Forget about her, though. I'ma make sure you get everything back. What you need to do right now is go home and get those bricks out the trunk of the white Benz in front of your mom's old house on Troy."

I eased back in my comfortable leather seat, wondering how the robbers had happened to catch me slipping just as I was leaving out with my duffle bag. I was also wondering why Kisha had not yet called me back with an apology. Usually, our arguments on the phone led to me hanging up mid-call and her calling back dozens of times until I answered or responded with a text message, and she *always* apologized, whether she was wrong or not.

So why wasn't my phone lighting up?

My thoughts shifted to the twenty-five kilos Lil Cholly had just mentioned. I knew that I could easily sell each for $30,000, which meant $450,000 at the end for me if I decided to give Royce his cut and $750,000 if I didn't.

"You got the keys to that Benz?" I asked, turning to Cholly with an indecipherable expression on my face.

Cholly frowned. "Keys?"

"Yeah, nigga! How the fuck I'm s'posed to open the trunk without a key?"

"Oh," Cholly said, opening his door, "he had a stripper chick drive it over there. She should be sittin' in the Benz waitin' on you. And man... wait till you see how thick *she* is."

Chapter 43

As soon as I turned off Roosevelt Road onto Kedzie, I immediately tucked the pistol inside the snug stash-box beneath my seat and lowered the volume on Twista's *Adrenaline Rush*; CPD cars were everywhere and driving around on 30-inch rims bumping gangster rap with a gun on my lap was a recipe for disaster.

I made a quick turn onto 13th and spotted the clean, white S550 Benz in front of my parents' old duplex in the middle of Troy Street. A caramel-toned girl in a tight black dress was standing on the porch with a phone to her ear. As I drove by, I saw what Cholly had already told me: the girl's ass was as big and round as Candice's.

Pulling over in front of the Benz, I found myself hoping the girl's face would be as stunning as her measurements.

She didn't disappoint.

Her flawless brown visage captivated me instantly. I watched her descend the concrete stairs, smiling nervously and waving at me. After retrieving the pistol from under my seat, I slid it into the waistline of my sweats and glanced around the block. Two police cars were parked at the corner of Roosevelt and Troy, and another was creeping down 13th.

I got out and gave the pretty girl a brief hug. "You're Mikey, right?" she asked.

I nodded.

"I'm Bubbles," she said. "Can we go inside until some of these police leave? I'm not about to open that trunk while they're out here stopping everybody."

"I gotta go in anyway," I said and walked around her incessantly flicking my eyes in every direction in search of any potential robbers.

The paralyzing memory of my father's dead body being carried out the front door assaulted me as soon as I glanced at the *FOR SALE/RENT* sign inside the front bedroom window. I kept walking, afraid that if I stopped for a mere few seconds to study the sign, I'd be shot dead. After a final look-around, I dug in my pocket for the house keys and unlocked the door.

"Who's the landlord over here?" Bubbles asked, following me in.

"Pops left it to my momma." I locked the door and trailed Bubbles into the empty, brown-carpeted living room. "Close those curtains. I gotta go grab somethin'. Got a place to sit in my bedroom back here."

I moved hurriedly down the short hallway, past my bedroom on the right and the bathroom on the left, and finally to my parents' old bedroom, which was adjoined to the kitchen. Like most of the building's rooms, it too was empty—aside from the AK-47 that was stretched out on the closet floor. I picked it up and went out to the kitchen.

Bubbles was leaning back against the wall across from my bedroom door doing something on her smartphone. All the bad luck I'd experienced since my father's murder had me leery of Bubbles already.

"Who you textin'?" I asked, yanking back the slide on my assault rifle to chamber a round from its 50-round banana clip.

Bubbles looked at the long gun, and then her pretty brown eyes shifted to mine. She dropped the phone into her black leather bag.

"Well," she said, "I *was* letting my girl know that this place is for rent, since she's been looking for somewhere to stay out this way. But never mind now." She crossed her arms and squinted at me. "You didn't have nothin' to do with Ton getting' killed, did you?"

"Ton got killed?" I put on a false look of surprise. "Damn, I ain't even know."

"Nigga, you know."

"No, I didn't. I was wonderin' what had all these cops out here. What's up with those blocks?" I led the way into my bedroom, sat at the foot of my bed, and turned on the television.

"Blocks?" Bubbles moved to the doorway, toying with the white diamond tennis bracelet on her wrist.

"The bricks," I said eying her matching necklace and hoop earrings, and her tall, black Gucci heels.

"Oh," she giggled softly. "The twenty-five bricks? They're in some old Macy's bags in my trunk, five kilos in each bag. And I know a few niggas you can get 'em off to. At least nine or ten bricks can go to your guy Tweet. He's been getting most of Lil Cholly's bricks for the past few months. Plus, most of the niggas I know from the club sell dope. A couple of phone calls and that shit'll be gone today."

Bubbles put a thumbnail between her teeth and displayed a slight smile. I felt her eyes on me as I flipped through channels with the TV remote, still trying to decide if I was going to pay Royce for the bricks.

"I hope you're planning on stopping by the club and throwing some of that money my way," Bubbles said. She leaned a shoulder against the doorframe and kept staring at me. "You know what?" she added, squinting again. "I heard about you. You're the young nigga off Trumbull who just came up last week; the nigga with the Monte Carlo on sixes, right? Is that Chevy outside yours, too?"

I regarded her with a suspicious frown.

"You ask too many questions." I stood and went to the window to peer through the blinds; the block seemed deserted, a sure sign that police were still in the area. I laid my assault rifle on the bed and turned to Bubbles. "How do you know me?"

"Ton..." Bubbles paused. "I met him at the club a while ago, back when I first started dancing. He called me a few days ago telling me he'd been jumped by you and some other niggas, said he was gon' catch y'all one at a time and fuck y'all up." She let out a brief chuckle and shook her head. "Guess that didn't work out for him."

"Yeah, I guess not. It's a cold game out here. Niggas been gettin' killed left and right. I'm thinkin' about leavin' Chicago once I get my money right."

"Nigga, you got good money. Every nigga King Royce deals with got *big* money, so I know you got it too. And you got the coldest old school Chevy I done seen parked in front of my Benz. Like I said—" she turned to the side and cupped her globe-sized derriere in both hands "—you know you wanna see me dance. Come through and make it rain. Drop five or ten thousand on a bitch. I'll give you a nice lil treat."

I looked out the window again, and for the first time since I'd been robbed, I smiled. Honestly, I could not help it. There was a steatopygic dime piece standing in my bedroom doorway, and though I knew it was my appearance—the Louis Vuitton and Rolex watch I was wearing, my Caprice on 30-inch rims—that had her captivated, I still felt good about it.

"Why I gotta go to the club to see you dance? You can dance for me right here," I said, motioning toward the bed.

"Nigga, do you think I'm stupid? Y'all finna be out here shootin' all day. Especially when Black Cory n'em find out about Ton. Be damned if I stick around to get shot." Bubbles checked her watch for the time. Then she looked me up and down and said, "Let's go to my house on Ridgeway. You can chill for a minute with me and my friend, and put those bags in your Chevy when you leave. Just follow me."

Without a bit of hesitation, I went to the Louis Vuitton suitcase beside my bed, pulled a large bath towel and two extra banana clips from inside it, draped the towel over the AK, and trailed Bubbles to the front door.

"See if the law still out there," I said, tucking the extra clips in my sweatpants pockets… and staring at Bubbles' big bubbles.

She backed into me as she opened the door, and we stayed that way while she stuck her head outside and scanned the street. The feeling of her big, soft ass against my sweats hardened me instantly. My phone began ringing, but I ignored it. Bubbles' Charmin soft curves held me captive.

"They're gone," she muttered gently. "Mmm, I can't wait to get you home. I feel that thing in your pants already." She shut the door and turned to face me. "You single?" she asked, biting her thumbnail again.

"I might be tonight," I replied as I slipped my free hand around her waist and squeezed her meaty butt . "What's your real name? And what kinda car Black Cory drive?"

"My name's Lakita. I used to date Bulletface, the rapper Alexus Costilla was engaged to. You actually kinda remind me of him."

I cracked another smile as I followed Bubbles out the door and to our cars at the curb. I tossed the AK-47 onto my passenger's seat, got behind the wheel, and started the engine. Lakita appeared at my window just as I cranked up the volume on Chief Keef's *I Don't Know Dem*.

"Black Cory drives a dark gray Maserati and a red Avalanche. He's usually alone in the Maserati, got some goons with him if he's in the Avalanche. Be careful." She leaned in through the window to kiss my cheek. "And you better be single, too."

I made a few phone calls during the brief drive to Lakita's place on 23rd and Ridgeway. I left Tyrone a voicemail warning him about Black Cory, checked on my mom and sister, and then phoned my big brother, Scrilla Man, and told him about the robbery.

"The bitch Lacresha was with the same niggas who shot up my Monte Carlo last week," I said.

"Aw, hell nah, you know I'm on the way out there with this choppa. I'm in Louisville with Rose and Smoke. We'll be on the highway in ten minutes." He paused for a moment, and then added, "Damn, and I was just about to come back to you. Niggas need eight."

What he meant was his conglomerate of Gangster Disciples in Indiana needed eight kilos of cocaine.

"Come on wit' it," I said, glad that Lil Cholly had plugged me with his connect.

I'd later learn a proverbial street lesson that I'd been hearing all my life: all money ain't good money.

Chapter 44

The shrill whip of a churning blender awakened Tyrone from a dream of being arrested for Ton's murder.

Reluctantly, he forced open his eyes and gritted his teeth at the irritating sound of the blender. Jessica was fast asleep beside him, seemingly impervious to the shrieking machine.

A web of pain sprouted in Tyrone's shoulder as he sat up and swung his legs over the bedside. The two week old bullet wounds in the upper left area of his chest and back made it difficult to move without suffering. He popped two extra-strength pain pills, shut his eyes, and waited for the powerful drug to kick in.

Seconds later, a knock at Jessica's bedroom door compelled Tyrone to open his eyes. He stood up, disconnected his smartphone from its charger, and went to the door in his boxers, turning on the phone as he went.

He opened the door and found a dozen young mobsters seated and standing around the living room. They were all wearing Louis Vuitton visor caps, big white t-shirts with *SICKO MOBB* printed across the chests in bold black letters, baggy denim jeans, and Jordan sneakers. The pistols in their laps and waists held 30-round magazines. The group consisted of most of Tyrone's closest friends, TVLs from his "Holy City" neighborhood who stood with him through thick and thin.

"Hurry up and get dressed, nigga. How much sleep you need?"

Joe-Joe said from his seat on the sofa. He was rolling a blunt, and there were four blunts already in rotation. "It's seven-thirty, Ty. We gotta be at Adriana's by nine for the show. I knocked on the door 'cause ol' girl want you in the kitchen."

"Ol' girl?" Tyrone asked, yawning.

"Kisha and her two sisters just got here a few minutes ago. Man, all of 'em lookin' *baaad* too. Wait till you see the redbone."

An uncomfortable silence followed. Everyone knew that Kisha was Mikey's girl. But to them, most girls were "thots"—promiscuous hood girls with seedy reputations. Neither of the TVLs cared about who the thots were fucking, especially since Mikey had been fucking Jessica, Tyrone's girl, for nearly a week now.

"And another thing," Joe-Joe continued, lighting his kush-filled White Owl blunt. He pointed his Glock at the living room window, coughed thrice, and said, "You ever seen a red Avalanche on Douglas before? 'Cause it's one parked down the street, been there all day. Ceno said he saw a bitch in the driver's seat."

Instinctively, Tyrone turned and dipped back into the bedroom. He grabbed his gun—a chrome .45 caliber Smith and Wesson with red laser sighting and a 30-round extended magazine—from under his pillow, put on the jeans and shoes he'd worn yesterday, and then cocked his pistol as he re-entered the living room.

"I'll be ready in 'bout fifteen minutes. Already got my outfit in the bathroom," Tyrone said, heading into the kitchen.

***

"You still shouldn't have set Mikey up," Kesa was whispering to Kisha as Tyrone walked into the small apartment's kitchen area.

The three sisters—Kisha, Kesa, and Candice—were all hunched over the circular wooden table, pouring cognac from their Hennessey bottles into red plastic cups. Kisha watched Tyrone's mouth fall agape as he admired their form-fitting designer mini-dresses, their Louboutin red- bottomed heels… and the thick bundle of cash in Kisha's left hand.

Kisha gave him a suggestive smile, biting down on her bottom lip.

His cold reply turned her smile upside down.

"The fuck y'all doin' over here? You know my girl in there sleep? Didn't I tell you to always call first?" His voice rose an octave with every question.

Kisha paused, frozen in place by Tyrone's icy words.

"Nigga," Candice cut in, "I went to Dvorak wit' Jessica. We came to turn up wit' that bitch, not you or yo' lil Sicko crew."

"We really did come to kick it wit' Jessica," Kisha said, lying through her teeth as she took a seat at the table and pulled a pack of playing cards out of the new Chanel bag she'd bought earlier that day, during her $20,000 shopping spree. "We came to play Spades, Ty. Ain't nobody chasin' yo' lil young ass."

"Yeah, a'ight," Tyrone said with a grin. He flicked his eyes from Kesa to Candice and back to Kisha. His gaze landed on the cash in Kisha's hand as she stuffed it back down inside her black leather bag. "Where you get all that money from?" he asked.

Kisha was thinking up another lie when Joe-Joe shouted from the living room, "If you don't getcho dirty ass in the shower!"

With a drab chuckle, Tyrone turned around, scrolling down the smartphone in his right hand and holding his perilous pistol in his left.

Kisha cast a salacious smile at the large HOLY CITY tattoo etched across the top of his back, and the twin mounds of cash jutting out of his back pockets. She liked him a lot, she decided; and the fact that he was close friends with Trav and Ceno—Sicko Mobb's top two rappers who had already been offered a three million dollar contract from Def Jam—made Kisha like Tyrone even more.

She watched him until he disappeared into the bathroom.

"Kisha you are so fucking stupid." Kesa sat down and took a sip of cognac. "First you set Mikey up, and then you bring us to *Mikey's* neighborhood so you can fuck his best friend? That's fucked up. And you know I'm a CPD officer now. I shouldn't be here in the first place. You're going to get me fired before I even start."

Kisha rolled her eyes. "Bitch, these niggas got money. I'm not about to be hangin' around no *broke* niggas." She started shuffling the cards, nervously bouncing her leg under the table as she struggled to come up with a remedy for the situation with Mikey.

Chapter 45

"Bruh, you get that voicemail I left you earlier?" I asked with a repressed groan.

I was sitting on Lakita "Bubbles" Thomas' large gray leather sofa, squeezing and rubbing her bountiful butt cheeks while she slurped my dick in and out of her mouth. We had been fucking on and off all day, halting only to eat and watch a movie. Her culinary skills were impeccable, and her sex was even better.

I had my phone to ear, my boxers and sweats pooled around my ankles, and my eyes on the wall-mounted 60-inch flat-screen television.

ESPN was on, but sports were not on my mind. I was focused on my money, making sure Tyrone and Joe-Joe were safe, and the twenty-five kilos of cocaine I'd moved from the trunk of Bubbles' Benz to the trunk of my Chevy earlier in the day.

"Yeah, but I ain't listened to it yet," Tyrone said. "I just woke up, bruh. 'Bout to hop in the shower and dip off to Trav and Ceno's show."

"Just be on the lookout for a gray Maserati or a red Avalanche, lil bruh," I warned. "And if you see that bitch Kisha out anywhere, check and see if she done come up on some extra money. I'm tryin' to make sure she didn't set me up."

"Wait a minute. You said a red Avalanche?"

134

"Yeah. That's Ton's people. Some nigga named Black Cory.

Why, you seen that truck?"

"It's parked down the street right now, big bruh."

"On Douglas?"

"Yup." He released a heavy breath that I heard through the phone, and then said, "Man, I know you gon' cuss me out about this shit… gotta tell you, though. Can't leave you in the dark."

A frown of suspicion locked my face. The expression remained as my scrotum tightened and my semen spurted up into Bubbles' steadily sucking mouth. I waited for Tyrone to continue.

"I fucked Kisha the other day, bruh. It was right before y'all smashed on Ton, when you was over there fuckin' Jessica."

"So what?" I said, hiding the pain. "Fuck that bitch. I'm done wit' her anyway. You still should've told me, but I ain't trippin'. Only thing on my mind is gettin' my bread back up. Pussy muhfuckas got me for everything."

"Kisha just came over here wit' her sisters, bruh. She got a fat ass bankroll on her too, looked like at least twenty racks."

My teeth grinded together, as I settled into a deep state of thought. Did Kisha set me up? Had she conspired with Lacresha, the stripper who'd been involved in and was now wanted for my father's murder?

A third, more profound question confronted me. Was Kisha in cahoots with King Royce, the man protecting Lacresha from my goons? The man who had just given me twenty-five kilos?

My eyes drifted to Bubbles' wobbling derriere as she got up, wiping the remains of my semen from her luscious lips. She sauntered to the bathroom, flitting her hips and gazing over her shoulder at me, and I briefly wondered if she would eventually betray me like Kisha had.

"You know what?" Tyrone continued. "Don't even trip, bruh. I'ma take care of that nigga Black Cory *and* this bitch Kisha. Feel like I did some fuck shit when I fucked Kisha anyway. I was really on her 'cause you fucked my lil bitch, but fuck these thots. We all we got. I'ma make it up to you. Lay low where you at. Fuck goin' to the Sicko Mobb concert, I'm out here."

"I'll be on Trumbull in about thirty minutes," I said, pulling up my boxers and sweatpants and grabbing my AK-47 from the thick, gray- carpeted floor.

"A'ight. If I'm not there"—Tyrone paused—"you know what happened."

"Solid, joe."

"Solid."

I ended the call and clipped the phone to my waistline, shaking my head as I envisioned Kisha and Tyrone fucking in my bed. I remembered the odd tension I'd sensed from them when I returned home that day. I remembered Kisha rushing off to the bathroom to brush her teeth, supposedly because she'd been drunk and vomiting before I walked in.

Had she really gone to brush her teeth for another reason? I gritted my teeth at the notion. "Nasty bitch," I muttered, stepping over to the living room window to peer through the gray vertical blinds.

My brother Scrilla Man's dark-blue Escalade was just pulling in behind my Chevy, and a white Mustang was idling across the street.

"My girl Shay should be back with my daughter any minute now," Bubbles said from the bathroom. "Let me know if you see a white Mustang out there."

"It's already here. And my big bruh just pulled up." I put on my shirt, slipped the AK-47 down inside the left leg of my sweatpants, and held it there as I opened the front door.

Hearing Bubbles mention her friend Shay reminded me of another Shay—Shay Cooper, the woman I killed a few days before for

136

stealing my brother's Escalade and all of our guns, drugs, and cash. Which is why I was shocked beyond belief when Shay Cooper came walking across the street with Bubbles ten-year-old daughter, Ra'Mya.

My brother and his cousin Rose-G got out of the Escalade carrying Gucci duffle bags. I glanced their way and saw that they were looking just as shock as I was. They had seen me shoot Shay in the face not even a week prior; yet here she was, still as sexy and skinny and pretty- faced as she'd been before I blew her brains out, wearing a forced smile and a black church dress as she walked up the porch steps. She stopped in front of me and opened her mouth to speak; my heart stopped.

"So let me guess," she said, grabbing her slender hips. "You're the reason Kita missed my sister's funeral."

"Huh?" I was at a loss for words.

"My twin's funeral was today," she explained. "I'm Lashay, her name was Cashay. Kita swore up and down she wouldn't be able to make it to the funeral 'cause she had some important business to handle. I knew she was lyin'."

Suddenly Bubbles was behind me. I stepped out onto the porch to let Lashay and Ra'Mya inside.

"I didn't lie," said Bubbles. "Royce paid me to drop somethin' off. You know I wouldn't've missed Cashay's funeral." She cut her eyes at me. "I can't say I didn't have some fun *after* the drop…"

I moved away from the girls and headed down the porch steps, firmly gripping the compact assault rifle in my pants and studying Scrilla Man and Rose's bewildered expressions as I approached them.

"Lil bruh, tell me that's not—" Scrilla Man started.

"It's not." I used the remote key to pop my Chevy's trunk.

"That's Lashay, her twin sister. I know; it fucked me up too." I looked at their duffle bags. "Is that the bread?"

"Yup. Ran it through the money machine twice after I counted it myself. Two hundred and forty thousand on the nose, and I'll be right back at you next month," Scrilla mumbled vacantly. He and Rose were still staring at Lashay in disbelief. "I want these duffle bags back too. Paid damn near two racks apiece for 'em."

After a lengthy visual sweep of the street, I opened the trunk. There were five kilos stacked in each of the five Macy's bags. I took two bricks out of one bag and tossed them to the side, and then handed the bag with the three kilos along with a bag with five kilos to Rose.

"That's the eight, bruh. And it's A-1 fish-scale. Straight from my nigga Lil Cholly's connect." I shut the trunk and took ahold of the two duffle bags. "Damn, I gotta put this shit up before I hit Douglas," I said, putting the duffles in my backseat while Rose went to stash the eight bricks somewhere inside the Escalade.

"What's wrong, lil bruh?" Scrilla asked. He could always tell when something was troubling me.

"The nigga we stomped out the other day came through earlier talkin' gunplay and got whacked. We gotta get his guys out the way. One of 'em parked on Douglas right now."

"Let's do it. I brought the fifty-shot Mac out to play." Without another word, Scrilla opened the driver's door of his SUV and climbed in, no doubt ready to squeeze off shots at whomever.

Bubbles had slipped back into her tight dress and heels. I watched her descend the stairs with her head down and thumbnail tucked between her pretty lips. I found myself suddenly captivated by her beautiful visage and her curvaceous figure. She walked up just as I was getting settled behind my Chevy's steering wheel.

"Are you coming back tonight? 'Cause I'm calling off work if you wanna stay the night," she said, planting her hands on her generous hips. "You know I'm really into you, right? I don't just fuck everybody."

I shut my door and gave Bubbles a slight grin. "I'm single now," I said, laying the AK-47 on the passenger's seat and starting the Caprice's powerful engine. "So yeah, I'll be back some time tonight. Have me a plate ready. No pork."

Chapter 46

Lacresha Radcliff's lips were mashing passionately against Two-One's, and her eyes were unwaveringly locked on the entrance to the apartment building across the street.

The two of them were standing on the sidewalk in front of the Johnson School of Excellence on Douglas Boulevard. They had their arms curled around each other's waists as if they were a loving couple, but there was no love or affection. Her hands were lingering near the .40 caliber Glock in the back of his pants, and his left hand was rubbing the nine millimeter Ruger on her right hip. Parked around the corner on Albany was the shiny red 4-door Audi coupe that King Royce had purchased for Lacresha just two days before. Treys was reclined in the Audi's passenger seat with a 120-round drum clipped into the AR-15 on his lap.

Separating her lips from Two-One's, Lacresha lifted her cell phone and dialed Kisha's number.

***

Kisha's phone was vibrating on the kitchen table when Tyrone emerged from the bathroom with his gun raised.

"All you hoes get naked *right* muhfuckin' now! Joe-Joe, get in here nigga!" Tyrone's tone of voice was an iceberg, and his gun was aimed at Kisha's head.

Apparently someone had fetched Jessica during Tyrone's hasty, five-minute shower. Kisha, her sisters, and Jessica were all sitting around the kitchen table with playing cards in their hands. Kisha's mouth dropped open as tears sprang forth from her eyes and a terrified gasp blew from her mouth.

"Bitch, y'all got five seconds!" Tyrone shouted.

Kisha started undressing in a hurry, peeling off her tight dress and kicking off her expensive heels. Candice hopped up and grabbed her hips, ready to argue.

"Girl, I ain't strippin' for these niggas unless I'm gettin' paid for it. And nigga, if you don't get that gun out my sister's face—"

Joe-Joe rushed into the kitchen and slapped his gun against Candice's forehead, grounding her mid-sentence and opening a gash that sent blood spilling down her gorgeous face. She screamed out in pain.

"Bitch, shut the fuck up!"

Tyrone made Jessica empty Kisha and her sister's designer bags onto the table. Inside them was just what he expected to find: tens of thousands of dollars in hundred-dollar bills, all rubber-banded in rotund bundles.

"You set my nigga up," Tyrone muttered.

"I'm *sorry!*" cried Kisha.

Just then, Way-Way, another TVL and Sicko Mobb member, entered the kitchen with his 30-round pistol in hand. "Bruh, what we on wit' these hoes? Trav and Ceno n'em just left for the show."

"They set Mikey up. And they was with the bitch that shot me last week and her lil guys, the same niggas who shot up Homan the other day," Tyrone said, his voice an incredulous whisper. "Bruh, stay here with these bitches for a minute. Joe-Joe, come on. We'll be right back." Tyrone turned and rushed down the short hallway with Joe-Joe trailing close behind him.

"Cuz, what the fuck goin' on? They set Mikey up?" Joe-Joe inquired.

"We got more important things to think about for now, lil cuz. We need to bang that Avalanche up. It's Ton's people."

"Say no more."

The two young mobsters sprinted across the now-empty living room and out the door.

Chapter 47

I was at a red light on Douglas and Kedzie when I spotted the red Avalanche... and the large, dark man who was crouched down beside its passenger door with an assault rifle in hand.

Further up the busy street, I saw Tyrone and Joe-Joe. They were just exiting their apartment building. I could see the guns in their hands and the long 30-round clips. I glanced over my shoulder at the two duffle bags in the back seat, and for the first time in a long while, I froze up. The possibility of me getting busted with seventeen kilos of cocaine and just under a quarter million in cash was a hard pill to swallow. But my loyalty to Tyrone far outweighed the fear of any prison sentence.

I parked my big orange box Chevy in the middle of traffic and stepped out with my AK-47.

"Black Cory," I shouted.

The man hunched down next to the Avalanche looked back at me. I opened fire.

***

"You killed my brother!" Lacresha screamed as she and Two-One pulled their guns and started firing at Tyrone and the kid who was walking out of the apartment building with him.

Tyrone quickly returned fire and ducked low beside a black Monte Carlo on massive chrome rims; his young comrade was not so lucky. The little guy's head jerked back when one of Two-One's bullets hit his face. His body shook as several more rounds penetrated his chest. He collapsed to the sidewalk and didn't move.

It was then that Lacresha noticed the heavy gunfire a block down, on Kedzie and Douglas. The deafening blasts frightened her half to death. She took off running around the corner to her car and nearly ran into Treys as he rushed to Two-One's side.

"He's on the other side of that black car," Cre yelled to Treys. "Hurry up and drop that nigga so we can go."

She got behind the wheel of her Audi, drove around the corner, and then watched in amusement as Treys unleashed his assault rifle on the black Monte Carlo across the street.

The explosions were earsplitting. The fiery glow of the AR-15's thunderous barrel had Lacresha shaking with a mixture of fear and excitement. Treys riddled the Monte Carlo's driver's side from front to back, shattering its windows and flattening its tires within seconds.

Chapter 48

Taking Black Cory's life was easier than taking candy from a baby. I managed to shoot him two or three times in the back as he scrambled around to the other side of his SUV for cover. He laid his rifle on the hood and sent a few rounds my way. People started screaming and running. Cars sped away from the gunfight. And I kept shooting.

Phop Phop Phop Phop Phop Phop Phop!

Scrilla and Rose were hanging out the Escalade, guns ablaze. A lady in a minivan nearly ran me over as she sped around my car to escape the brazen shootout... which is when I noticed, out of the corner of my eye, that there were also guns blazing across the street from where Tyrone and Joe-Joe had been standing seconds earlier. I had to get down there, and fast... even if it meant risking my own life.

Bravely — or perhaps "foolishly" is a better word for the situation — I jogged over to the rear of the Avalanche, paused for a second or two, and then stepped out into the street. I found Black Cory lying on his stomach in a burgeoning pool of blood. He was attempting to crawl away but his legs and arms were too riddled with bullet wounds. A three-round burst from my AK-47 gave his head the appearance of a smashed tomato.

"Lil bruh, you good?" Scrilla Man asked as he ran up behind me.

"Yeah, I'm good. Y'all need to be on the highway wit' them thangs, bruh. Love," I said, running back to my Caprice.

The Escalade's tires screeched as Scrilla Man took off down Kedzie.

I stomped on the gas and raced forward on Douglas just as someone in front of the school on the corner of Douglas and Albany started firing off what sounded like a machine gun.

Closing in, I realized that the two dread-headed teens shooting Tyrone's car up were the same guys Lacresha had brought along to rob me that morning. One of them—the one holding the rifle—glanced at my Chevy as I barreled up the boulevard toward them. I was driving much too quickly for them to fully react to what was about to happen. I swerved onto the sidewalk, pushed my back against my seat and coiled my fingers tightly around the steering wheel.

Then I hit them.

One gunman—the lighter of the two—webbed my windshield as he tumbled up the hood and over the roof. The second goon went flying into the driver's door of a red Audi that was idling at the corner.

I hit the brakes and veered sharply to the left, avoiding a collision with the Audi. Then I raced across the street and stopped at the corner next to Tyrone's apartment building.

Tyrone was on his back beside the Monte Carlo and Joe-Joe was stretched out the same way on the sidewalk. Both of them were bleeding profusely. Neither of them was moving.

Police sirens sounded in the distance.

Then came a gunshot from inside the apartment building.

"The fuck is goin' on?" I murmured, checking my rearview mirror to make sure the two gunmen were still grounded.

They were... and the red Audi was now right behind my Chevy.

Suddenly, Lacresha Radcliff's pretty face was outside my passenger window. I saw a bright flash, heard a stentorian bang.

And then there was darkness.

Chapter 49

"He's moving! Is he awake? Mikey, can you hear me?" My mother's soothing voice was replete with worry.

I forced open my right eye and inhaled deeply. Looking around the clean white hospital room, I wondered why I was there. I could not remember being hurt.

'Why do I have such a splitting headache?' I thought.

"Mikey? Mikey, can you hear me?" Momma was leant over the side of my bed, cradling my hand in hers. She was dressed in a Bears t-shirt and jeans, and her hair was a wreck.

"I can hear," I murmured, lifting my other hand to massage my sore throat. "What happened?"

"Somebody shot you, Michael; took out your left eye. Kisha drove you here, so you need to be thanking her when you get up and moving."

"How long I been out?" I touched my face and felt gauze over my left eye.

"They kept you asleep until the swelling in your brain lessened. It's been two weeks and a day now."

'Two weeks! What the fuck happened?'

I flicked my eye around the room. Kisha was asleep beneath a blanket in the easy chair next to my bed. A Tyler Perry movie was playing on the television.

"Kisha," I tried speaking in a regular tone, but only a hoarse whisper escaped.

She heard me.

"Mikey!" She stood up in a hurry and rushed to my side. "I'll go and find the doctor," Momma said, turning to leave.

Kisha pressed her lips against mine the moment my mother left the room. A tear fell from her eye onto my cheek.

"I'm so sorry, Mikey. It's all my fault. I take full responsibility for everything. *Please* forgive me." She sat down next to me, studying my face and rubbing a hand over the chest of my hospital gown. She too was dressed comfortably in jeans and a t-shirt, and her hair was pulled back in a ponytail.

"Just tell me… what happened," I muttered hoarsely.

"I don't even know where to start. It was all so crazy." Kisha buried her face in her palms and shook her head. "Way-Way was holding us at gunpoint in the kitchen, arguing with Kesa 'cause she wouldn't take offher clothes. We started hearing a bunch of gunshots outside. Kesa whipped out that gun she always keeps strapped to her thigh when we go out, and she shot Way-Way. Then we got all our stuff off the table and ran outside. Found you in your car, covered in blood. Kesa helped me get you into the backseat. I took your place in the driver's seat and drove you here. I've been here with you every night since then. And don't worry; all that stuff from your car is put up at my new apartment. I haven't told anybody about it."

I cleared my throat and stared at the TV. Madea was chain- sawing a couch in half. My memory was slowly returning. I remembered being robbed by that maniacal woman Lacresha and her two goons. I remembered breaking up with Kisha shortly afterwards, though the reason eluded me.

Just then, Kisha said something that took me away from my thoughts, something that made me cringe with sadness.

"I went to Tyrone and Joe-Joe's funeral last week; didn't go to Way-Way's. Oh, and I put money on Scrilla Man and Rose's books. Ended up paying fifteen thousand altogether for their lawyers. They got pulled over and busted with some guns and eight bricks of coke on the highway in Indiana. Somebody who was on Douglas that night reported your brother's license plate number to the police, said they witnessed him and Rose kill that dude on Kedzie and Douglas."

Kisha turned to look at me and I saw that she was still crying. I reached out and gave her hand a reassuring squeeze…

Chapter 50

One Week Later

"Your guy out of the hospital yet?" "Yeah. I ain't seen him though." "Got his phone number?"

"Yeah, I already called like four or five times. It's going straight to voicemail. I'ma call his mom today."

"I need my money, Lil Cholly."

"I know. Mikey gon' pay for that shit. He ain't the type to be runnin' off wit' nobody's bread."

"Let's hope not," Royce replied.

***

I awoke that warm August morning with an empty stomach and a full erection. The bedroom door was wide open.

I got up and headed into the kitchen in my boxers. Candice was washing dishes in the sink; she ignored me as I grabbed a gallon of milk and a box of Frosted Flakes to eat. Setting the cereal and milk on the table, I stared at Candice's tight little boy shorts and wondered what she was doing here.

"Kisha just took some girl named Crystal to a doctor's appointment, said she'll be back in an hour or so."

With a devious grin, I walked up behind her and gave her a hug, pressing the tip of my rock-hard muscle against her meaty butt cheeks. She didn't resist, so I snaked a hand around her waist and into the front of her shorts.

No panties.

My middle finger slipped easily into the warm folds of her wet pussy.

"Didn't you put me out yo' car? Getcho hands off me, Mikey," She said softly as I pushed her shorts down to her knees.

"Shut up," I said, kissing the side of her neck as I freed my erection and guided it between her pillowy cheeks. "I still think y'all set me up. Anyway, you deserved that shit, just like you deserve this." I was already sliding in and out of her warm, creamy center with my hands clamped on her narrow waist.

"We didn't... set you..." were the only words Candice managed to get out before she dropped the bowl she'd been rinsing and succumbed to the intense pounding I had in store for her.

We went from the counter to the table and then to the floor, which is where we stayed until I pulled out and sprayed her inner thigh.

***

I showered, ate, and was in the vacant lot next to the house, cleaning out my new black Suburban when Kisha pulled up in her equally new black Range Rover. I'd taken the six 12" speakers out of my Caprice and put them in the Suburban. I had the volume on low, bumping Chief Keef's "Chiefin Keef," and it was still loud enough to shake the block.

We were now staying at 1530 S. Trumbull Avenue, smack dab in the middle of Holy City, land of the Vice Lords. It was America's fifth most dangerous neighborhood, a place where gunshots were as common as rain in April. The block was already alive at 9:00 a.m. Everybody had on RIP shirts for Tyrone, Joe-Joe, and Way-Way. My workers were in the alley serving fiends. Perk and Rev were barbecuing across the street.

"You're up early," Kisha said as she walked up and gave me a hug. "I just ran into Tweet on Cermak. He said he'll be back at you sometime today for another brick. And my girl Tyreeka's brother gave me eight thousand for another nine piece."

She took the $8,000 out of her Birkin bag and gave it to me. I dropped it in one of the back pockets of my baggy True Religion jeans. My eye wandered down Kisha's snug-fitting gray mini-dress and then back up to her pretty chocolate face. I did not trust her one bit. I'm sure she knew that much. But thanks to all the hustlers she'd gotten acquainted with while dancing at Arnie's, I now had less than a kilo left to sell and over $750,000 cash stashed inside Uncle Mutulu's condominium. Right now I needed Kisha.

Not for long, though.

"Why are you looking at me like that?" Kisha suddenly asked.

"Like what?" I smiled and adjusted the black patch over my left eye. "I got two nine pieces wrapped up in the freezer, just grab one. I'll let Tweet Body know it's over until I re-up."

"Did my sister leave?"

"Nah, she in there sleep."

She squinted at me for a second. "Where are you hiding all that money?"

"Last time I told you that, you gave a nigga the address and got me robbed for damn near a half million. Think I'm 'bout to do that again?"

"Are you going to hold that over my head forever? You can't be holding money in secret places when we get married."

'Married?' I almost laughed. There was no way I was going to marry Kisha after she had fucked Tyrone behind my back.

I leaned into the Suburban and turned up the volume. Kisha turned and stormed into the house.

Chuckling aloud, I sat in the driver's seat, lit a blunt, and started counting through the $8,000. I was almost done when Lil Cholly pulled up in his white Panamera and blew the horn.

I slipped the 30-round clip into my .40-caliber Glock and cocked a bullet into the chamber. After what had happened to Tyrone and Joe-Joe at the hands of Lacresha's goons, I'd decided against paying King for the bricks, and I was ready for whatever came with my decision.

Lil Cholly walked over and got in next to me. I passed him the blunt.

"What's up Lord?" he said as we shook hands. "You know dude pressin' me about that bread. If you don't pay that nigga, we gon' be at war with the Latin Kings."

"Well, we goin' to war. Fuck that nigga. I ain't payin' a dime. That bitch he fuck wit' got my lil niggas killed. I'm ready to die, too. Fuck everybody."

Lil Cholly shook his head. He put the blunt to his lips and pulled. I wondered how much the big diamonds in his ears and pinky ring had cost. I knew his diamond filled Rolex cost a helluva lot more than my rose gold one. He had been in the big money league for years already, and I was just now starting.

"That ain't a smart decision, Mikey. Think before you act. We just lost three Travs a couple of weeks ago, three good young niggas. The hood can't afford to lose no more. Shit, we getting' money now. Sicko Mobb got the whole hood turnt up. We had Twista out here for a video shoot the other day. All you gotta do is pay for the bricks, get twenty-five more, and keep flippin' that shit."

I hit the blunt and watched my nigga Lil Mark serve a crack- head in the alley. Lil Cholly was right. I needed to chill, lie back, and get money. But with all the drama I'd gone through since my father's murder, I was finding it hard to think.

"I'ma hit you later, bruh," I said, starting the engine. "Let me think this shit over. I'll be at you in a few hours."

"Solid, joe," Cholly said.

"Solid."

He got out and I drove off.

Chapter 51

King smiled at the shiny white Rolls Royce as it cruised into his circular driveway and parked next to his long black Benz. He was watching from an upstairs window inside his four-million-dollar Bellwood mansion. He donned a gray Versace suit and tie. His wife, Aesha, was standing beside him in a black Versace dress and Zanotti heels, sipping from a stem glass of white wine.

A second, longer Rolls Royce appeared at the wrought iron gate at the front of King's property, followed by four white Tahoes.

"It's really them," Aesha murmured. She sounded shocked.

"Yup," King nodded. "It's definitely them. Go and make some drinks. I'll bring them to the family room."

He headed down the glass spiral staircase, feeling nervous but not showing it. A few of his fellow Latin Kings were stationed both inside and outside the front door just in case things went sour, but he wasn't really expecting trouble. He had no idea why the billionaire Mexican drug cartel family's bosses had set up a meeting with him, but it had to mean more money, more kilos of cocaine and heroin, and more pounds of high-grade marijuana.

King rubbed his hands together excitedly.

The men stepping out of the Tahoes looked like CIA agents— black suits, dark shades, ear pieces, high-tech assault rifles, the whole nine. Two pretty mixed girls in short white dresses and matching heels got out of the second Rolls and breezed toward the mansion. King opened the tall French door and invited them into the family room.

"Have a seat. My wife's getting some drinks together now," he said, gazing lustfully at the girls' generous curves. They were as thick- bottomed and beautiful as Tahiry Jose. They had green eyes and long, curly, black hair. The biggest white diamonds King had ever seen were wrapped around their necks.

The girls sat on the large, gray, leather sofa and crossed their legs.

"We, uhh... need your help," said the shorter of the two. "I'm Mercedes Costilla. This is my sister, Alexus." King's mouth dropped open.

Mercedes Costilla! Alexus Costilla!

He couldn't believe it. The daughters of Mexico's most ruthless cartel boss were sitting right in front of him, in *his* house, and they needed *his* help.

He crossed his arms over his chest and gave a slow nod.

"You see," Mercedes said, "my sister is engaged to Blake..."

"Bulletface, right? The rapper. I read about it."

"Yeah. Well, there's this guy on the west side of Chicago who kidnapped Blake's daughter a while back. My sister wants him dealt with. The thing is, he's practically untouchable. We can get to him, but it'll get too messy and we'd lose some men in the process. What we need is somebody close to him to take him out. Think you can get it done?"

King cupped his chin in his hand and squinted thoughtfully.

Aesha came in with the drinks: Ciroc on ice. He had her set the stem glasses on the table and leave.

"So what's his name?" King asked.

"Some people call him Red-D," Alexus said, "but mostly everybody calls him Reesie Cup, or Cup for short. He's chief of the Traveling Vice Lords in the Lawndale neighborhood, owns that strip club on 16th Street and another club on Chicago Avenue."

King nodded again. "I know him. He's real close with Lil Cholly. I met him a couple of times."

"Can you get it done?" Mercedes asked.

"Depends," King said, pacing a tight circle in front of the fireplace. "What's in it for me?"

"A thousand bricks of coke, ten million cash, and lower prices." Alexus got up, shrugging her shoulders. "Hell, I'll give you fifteen million. Just get it taken care of."

King's mouth watered at the thought of the wealth he'd gain for the hit. He could sell the bricks cheap, $14,000 to $16,000 apiece, and still clear a good $14 million. Add the $15 million in cash and King would be the Windy City's reigning drug kingpin. His hustle was already legendary among the Latin Kings, but he wanted to be number one. 'Nobody remembers a number two kinda gangsta' is what his Uncle Herb had raised him to believe. 'The real gangstas are always in first place.'

He walked the girls and their bodyguards outside and stood in the doorway as they departed in their sparkling white Rolls Royces. His wife appeared at his side a moment later.

"My God... that was Alexus Costilla," Aesha muttered. "She's like Bill Gates rich. The Costillas own television networks and everything."

"Yeah. I know." King was thoughtfully holding his chin again. He needed someone close to Cup to get in and get the job done. Cholly was too loyal to Cup, so he wasn't an option.

But King had an idea...

He turned to his loyal King brothers and gave the order.

Chapter 52

I gave the door five quick knocks.

"Who is it?"

"Mikey."

Bubbles was already smiling widely when she swung the door open. She had on a t-shirt and pink sweatpants. Her hair was long and straight, obviously professionally done. She hugged me, and her perfume lingered.

"Crazy ass boy," she said as she pulled me in and shut the door.

"Told you I was coming back," I beamed.

"That was three weeks ago. And I heard about all that shootin' y'all did on Kedzie when Black Cory and those other boys got killed. My girl was right there at the light when it went down." Her eyes gave me a brief head to toe exam. "I like your Jordans," she added.

"Thanks. But I went home when I left here; wasn't even there when Black Cory got whacked."

"Mhm... I just bet you wasn't." She planted her hands on her hips, poking her lips out in disbelief.

I felt an overwhelming urge to kiss those sexy lips, but I held back.

"Come on, have a seat," she said.

Eye glued to her tremendous derriere, I trailed Bubbles into the living room. Her daughter was sitting Indian-style on the sofa with a pillow on her lap and a bottle of nail polish shaking in her little brown hand.

"Momma, why that man got a patch on his eye?" Ra'Mya asked immediately.

"Find you some business, lil girl." Bubbles plopped down on the sofa and put her bare feet on the pillow in Ra'Mya's lap. I sat next to her, and she leaned back across my lap, gazing up at me with those irresistibly kissable lips poked out again. "Please tell me there's an eye under that patch. The girls at the club said you got shot in the face, but I never heard where exactly."

"You are just as nosy as your daughter," I said.

"No, I'm not."

"Yes, she is," Ra'Mya said. "Where you think I got it from?"

Bubbles raised a foot to attack, but her daughter knocked it away and fell to the side laughing. I chuckled as she started fighting Ra'Mya with her foot. The little girl rolled off the sofa and hit the floor in a fit of jubilant laughter.

"Go upstairs and finish cleaning up that bedroom," Bubbles snapped. "If it's not done by eleven o'clock, we ain't going to McDonald's. And I'm not taking you to Grandma's either."

In one fluid motion, Ra'Mya grabbed her hips, rolled her eyes, twisted her neck, and sucked her teeth. I chuckled again; she glowered at me, and said, "You know this is your fault, right? I was getting' ready to paint her stinky lil toenails before you showed up."

"My toes don't stink," Bubbles said, grinning at her miniature look-alike.

"Yes they do, Ma. Your feet smell like stale French fries."

I cracked up laughing so hard that it ached my wounded eye. Bubbles sat up and threw the pillow at Ra'Mya, who took off running up the stairs, laughing harder than I was.

"I can't stand that lil brat sometimes." Bubbles dropped her head back onto my lap and smiled up at me. "Mind if I lay here for a minute?" She shut her eyes and let out a deep breath. "I got off work at four o'clock this morning and woke up at seven to feed the brat. Now she wants McDonald's, and to go over my mom's for a sleepover with her cousins."

Bubbles sighed and kept her eyes closed. I stared at the crotch of her sweatpants and licked my lips. She obviously wasn't wearing panties.

I couldn't help it. I lifted the front of her sweats and was just about to dig in when she popped open her eyes and slapped my hand.

"Not while my baby's here. She'll sneak halfway down the stairs just to look down and spy on us."

"Well, let's go to your bedroom," I suggested. My dick was swelling rapidly in my jeans, as if it had one of those gas station automatic air pumps attached to it. I knew Bubbles felt it throbbing behind her head.

"I know that's not what I think it is," she giggled, regarding me with the most beautiful smile I'd ever seen. "You are not about to be treating me like I'm just some booty call, Mikey. I want a little romance, too. Take me out on a nice date or something, or take me on a trip."

"I'll take you wherever you wanna go," I said, and I meant every word. There was something about Lakita "Bubbles" Thomas that had me intrigued, drawn in like a moth to a flame. Sure, she had the kind of ass that no black man would ever tire of seeing, but there was something I saw in her eyes that had me hooked.

We got up and went to her bedroom. The covers on the bed were red like the curtains on the window and the carpet on the floor. There was a large mirror on the ceiling over the bed and several more on the walls; I planned on putting them to use as soon as possible.

She sat on the side of the bed and lay back, shutting her eyes again. Then came another sleepy sigh. I locked the door and crossed the room to stand over her.

"You're going to McDonald's for Ra'Mya if you put me to sleep," Bubbles threatened as I slid her sweatpants off.

"I ain't got a problem with that." I pushed her thick thighs apart and kneeled between them, eyeing her plump, glistening wet pussy. "Let me eat some of this McBubbles' first," I said, spreading open her juicy vaginal lips and digging my tongue in deep for a quick taste.

She was delicious.

I moved up and sucked her clit. She put her hands on my head and started moaning, slowly winding her hips. The sweet scent of her juices had my dick straining against my zipper. I pushed in one finger, then two, and kept sucking and flicking my tongue across her clitoris until she slammed her thighs shut on my head.

"Wait, wait, wait... mmm, stop, I'm..." She tried to push my head away and scoot back across the bed but I was relentless.

I grabbed her thighs and ran my tongue up and down her tasty pussy, licking up the escaping juices. Once her orgasm had faded, I kissed my way up to her neck, snatching off my "RIP Tyrone" t-shirt.

"Please... do me a favor," Bubbles said breathlessly.

"What kinda favor?"

"Don't ever do that again."

"Do what?"

"Don't keep eating it when I'm coming. I can't take it. I'll be stalking you at two in the morning." She laughed softly.

I grinned down at her, unbuckling my Louis Vuitton belt. I took the Glock off my hip and the 30-round clip out of my front pocket and laid them on the bed, then took off my jeans and boxers.

"I'ma do it every time then," I said, slowly easing my rigid pole into her slippery pussy.

It was just as tight and warm as I remembered it to be. I fed her my entire length, slowly at first, then with quick thrusts that had her mouth and eyes wide open and her breaths escaping in short, heavy huffs.

I kissed her lower lip, sucked it into my mouth. She dug her fingernails into my back as I pounded in and out of her.

I lifted her shirt and yanked down the cups of her bra. Her breasts were just big enough to fill my hands, which is what I did, squeezing and sucking them passionately.

My mouth moved from her breasts to her neck and back to her breasts again. I realized that I wanted to suck and kiss and touch on her beautiful body forever.

Then the doorknob started twisting and turning.

The two of us paused just as my semen began spurting out inside her. A low grunt crawled out of my throat.

"Ma! Open up this door. I can't find my other sock," Ra'Mya shouted.

"Lil girl, if you don't get away from my door talkin' about a sock. Go up there and look for it." Bubbles was breathing hard like I was and we had only been going at it for a good ten minutes or so.

"I *did* look for it," Ra'Mya insisted, still working the doorknob. "I found this one under the bed, but the other one ain't there. I have looked everywhere. I checked the closet, looked in all my drawers, behind the dresser—can't find it, Ma. You gotta help me."

"I'll buy you some more socks, okay, Ra'Mya?"

"They're my favorite socks, Ma. You can't just buy a pair of favorite socks."

I stood and pulled up my boxers and jeans, laughing at the insane little girl's antics. Bubbles was shaking her head and smiling.

"Did you check the dryer? I washed some of your clothes with mine last night and put them in the dryer before I left." Bubbles sighed at the sound of her daughter's retreating footsteps. She cocked her head to the side and looked at me.

"What?" I smiled.

"Nigga, you know what. You didn't pull out."

"I couldn't… felt too good."

She rolled her eyes, groaned as she got up, and grabbed a box of Kleenex off the bedside table. I snatched out a few tissues and wiped myself off while Bubbles eased back on the bed, spread her legs, and forced the cum out of her pussy.

"Hope you know I don't believe in abortions, so if you get me pregnant…"

"I ain't trippin'. I want a son anyway." I took the $8,000 I'd gotten from Kisha out of my back pocket and tossed it to Bubbles. "You said I need to take you on a trip. That's eight racks; book the trip."

She dropped the soggy tissues in the trashcan next to the bed and put her sweatpants back on. "Where do you wanna go?" she asked, taking the rubberbands off the thick stack of hundreds and fifties.

"I don't care. Wherever you wanna go."

"What about the Bahamas? We can take one of those week-long cruise ship rides. It'll take us to a few different islands, like Turks and Caicos."

"I ain't gettin' on no ship. We can fly to Turks and Caicos or the Bahamas if you want to, but I ain't fuckin' wit' no ships."

"Why not? You scared of water?"

"Give me my money back," I said, putting the Glock on my hip and the long clip in my pocket.

"Okay, okay… I'll book the flight for this weekend." Bubbles went to her closet and stuffed the cash in a purse on the shelf. "Do you realize we haven't even exchanged numbers yet?" She turned and walked to me, placing one hand on her hip and extending the other. "Hand me your phone… so I can lock my number in."

I didn't trust her intentions. I suspected she wanted to peruse my messages and contacts to discern if I was dating other women, but I gave her my phone anyway.

"Okay, who the fuck is Kisha?" Bubbles asked a moment later.

"A nobody; I'll cut her off right now. Got most of my clothes at the condo anyway. She can have all that shit at the house on Trumbull." I put on my t-shirt and dipped my head forward to kiss Bubbles' lips. "I think that bitch set me up that day I met you; but she saved my life, drove me to the hospital when I got shot in the face. That's the only reason I got wit' her when I got out the hospital; ain't been but a week and a half.

"Nuh-uh, I'm deleting this bitch. Who is Alycia?"

"Ex... you can delete her too."

"Mhm, and Treecy?"

"That's my sister Latrice." I grinned at her harshness.

"It better be. Matter of fact, I wanna meet her... as soon as possible. And who is—wait, somebody just sent you a text."

"Let me see." I grabbed the phone and dropped it in my pocket.

Then I lifted Bubbles' chin with the side of an index finger and stared into

her pretty brown eyes. "As long as you keep it a hundred wit' me, you'll get the same treatment. A'ight? You can trust me. Shit, I *need* somebody to trust. My big bruh in the feds, my lil niggas dead. I think my bitch set me up. And with the kinda money I got now, I can't trust no nigga. I'm a gangsta nigga like my daddy was, but he had my momma holdin' him down until the day he got killed. I just want somebody to hold me down like that."

"I'll be all of that. But uuummm"—she moved my hand from her chin and pointed at the pocket I'd dropped my phone in—"don't you think we need to see that message?"

My mouth stretched into another grin. Bubbles was going to be a handful.

I dug the phone out of my pocket and immediately frowned at the unfamiliar number the text was sent from. It was a picture message. I opened it and my frown deepened.

It was a picture of my mom and sister. They were getting in Latrice's gray Impala, seemingly unaware that their picture was being taken.

The text beneath the picture made me grit my teeth in anger.

'Love them? THEN GIVE ME MY FUCKING MONEY! CALL ME!!'

Chapter 53

My knees went limp; I sat down on the bed and stared at the picture on my phone screen.

"That was King's number, wasn't it?" Bubbles asked.

I dialed Treecy's number. It rang five times, and my heart slammed harder and harder in my chest with every ring.

"Hey bro. What's up?" Latrice finally answered.

"Y'all okay? Where momma at?" My questions rushed out quicker than I intended them to.

"Boy, will you calm down? The hell wrong with you? I told you I was takin' her out to eat before we go shoppin' today."

"Where y'all at?"

"At Great Aunt Micki's, that new black-owned restaurant on Michigan Avenue."

"I'll be there in about twenty-five minutes. Don't leave without me," I ended the call.

Bubbles stood in front of me with her hands on her hips. I went back to the message and read it again.

"Did you ever pay King for all that dope I dropped off to you?" Bubbles asked.

"Nope." My left leg was bouncing uncontrollably. "I'm about to pay him. Then I'm blowin' his muhfuckin' head off." I dialed the number the text had come from, chewing my thumbnail to pieces and cursing myself for neglecting to pay King for the kilos. I'd put my family in danger. Momma and Treecy meant more to me than any amount of money. What the hell had I been thinking?

He didn't answer my call. I tried twice more and got the same result.

"I gotta go," I said, standing up.

"Where are you going?"

"Some restaurant on Michigan Avenue, Great Aunt Micki's." I unlocked the door and started to open it, but Bubbles slammed it shut and leaned back against it. "Listen Bubbles, I gotta go. This nigga done threatened my family. I don't play about my fam."

"Okay, well, you should have paid him… simple as that… business is business. Let me call and talk to him. I've known King Royce for about a year now. He'll listen to me, we'll get his money to him, and that'll be that. Now will you wait a minute so I can get some panties and shoes on?"

"I'll be in my truck."

Reluctantly, she stepped aside and I snatched open the door.

Ra'Mya was standing there holding up a pink and white sock with the face of a black princess printed all over it.

"Found it!" Ra'Mya was all smiles.

I stepped around her and crossed the living room to the front door, but Ra'Mya was tugging at the back of my shirt before I could grab the doorknob.

"Hey, Mr. One-Eye."

I turned and looked down at her. She had braids that zigged and zagged all across her scalp. Her shirt was black with JORDAN written on the chest; it matched her red jeans and Jordan sneakers.

"Did you really get shot in the eye?" She scrunched up her face. "*Ooooh*, I bet that *hurt*, didn't it? Did you go to the doctor? You got, like, a fake eyeball or somethin' under that patch?"

"Ay, stop askin' about my eye. A'ight? You ask too many questions."

"Don't get mad at me 'cause you ain't got no eye."

"Anybody ever told you that you got a smart mouth?"

"Yup. I'm the smartest kid in all my classes. A's in every class, and I made honor roll two years in a row. Bet *you* never made honor roll. I don't even know how you can read wit' no eye—well, one eye. I wouldn't be able to read like that."

Just then, Bubbles rounded the corner, holding her iPhone. She high-fived her daughter. "Wait a second; I'm calling King Royce now. And thanks, boo-boo."

"Anytime, Momma," Ra'Mya said, pinching her little gold earring and staring up at me with a terribly guilty smile.

It was my turn to scrunch up my face. I looked at Bubbles. "What did you do, tell her to keep me from leaving?"

The corners of her lips rose into the exact same smile Ra'Mya was wearing. She held up an index finger, and then pointed to the phone at her ear.

"Hello. Hey, it's Bubbles. I'm with Mikey. Can I put you on speakerphone so you two can… Hello? Hello?" Bubbles glanced at her phone screen. "He hung up on me," she muttered in disbelief.

Then my phone rang in my pocket.

Pulling it out, I saw that it was the unfamiliar 708 number. I put the phone to my ear.

"We need to meet," he said. I was surprised at how black he sounded. With him being a Latin King, I had expected a gruff Hispanic voice.

"First off, nigga," I said, taking a seat on the third step of the carpeted staircase that led to the second floor, "ain't nobody stole from you. You fronted me that shit; I didn't ask for it. And second, it ain't been nothin' but three weeks. I gotcho bread already, nigga. I ain't wit' the threats though."

"We need to meet," he repeated. "Where you wanna meet?"

"There's a nice soul food restaurant on Michigan Avenue, Great Aunt Micki's. I'll be waiting."

I was at my Suburban ten seconds later.

Chapter 54

It took every bit of restraint in me not to speed through the red lights on Roosevelt Road. Five minutes into the trip, I checked my rearview mirror and spotted Bubbles three car-lengths behind me, whipping her clean white Mercedes like a pro stunt driver. I made a few calls to the guys on 15ᵗʰ and Trumbull. My mind was racing faster than the Suburban. Pulling up in front of the opulent restaurant, I scowled at King's black Benz; it was parked right behind my sister's Impala.

I was tempted to take the 16-round magazine out of my Glock, slide in the 30-round clip, and barge into the restaurant on some gangsta shit. But I couldn't, not with Momma and Treecy there.

I pushed open my door and stepped out into what felt like a hundred degrees of heat. Bubbles was parking in the only available spot halfway down the busy street, but I didn't wait for her.

I took a deep breath, straightened my fitted cap, and entered Great Aunt Micki's wearing the calmest expression I could muster.

Momma and Treecy were laughing about something at a table near the large front window, and I suspected the guy in the business suit a few tables over was King.

I walked over and put a hand on Momma's shoulder. "Y'all okay?" I asked.

"Nope," Treecy replied. "We need help with this eighty-dollar bill we gotta pay. And I need you to lend me three hundred for this month's rent."

"I gotchoo; give me a minute. I gotta holla at my guy right quick." I looked at the door as Bubbles came walking in with Ra'Mya at her side. "That's my new girlfriend right there, Momma, in the pink sweatpants."

I motioned for Bubbles to sit at the table with Momma and Treecy, knowing they would keep her busy with their standard line of questions.

Then I turned and approached the table where the man in the business suit was sitting. He nodded to the seat across from him, and I sat down.

"So," he said, grinning and leaning back in his chair, "we finally meet." He studied my eye-patch for a moment. "I see Lacresha wasn't lying about shooting you in the face. Just to let you know, she's in Vegas now, so you don't have to worry about that crazy bitch anymore. Those two guys you ran over are laying somewhere in Cook County Jail's medical wing with a hundred broken bones, facing double murder charges, so you don't have to worry about them either. And by the way, I was one hundred percent uninvolved in that whole beef. She wanted your guy dead for killing her brother. I can't blame her for getting it done."

I moved forward and planted my elbows on the table, canted my head to one side, and stared contemptuously. *'This nigga can't be serious,'* I thought, but I didn't say a word. I had no words to give.

"You always this quiet?" he asked. Again, I said nothing.

"Mikey... I like the way you move in the streets. I've heard a lot about you. Word is, you've been putting in a lot of work out there on that west side. That's why I fronted you that much product. You don't think I'd just do that for anybody, do you? Of course I wouldn't. When Lil Cholly wanted out, he suggested you take his place, said you were serious about your money and quick to pull that trigger.

That's the kinda guy I need on my team right now, Mikey; the kinda guy that'll *kill* for some money. You with me so far?"

My teeth were clenched so tightly together that my head began to hurt, which is probably the only reason I opened my mouth to speak.

Keeping my voice calm and low was a struggle.

"Nigga, I'm not with you on nothin'! You followin' my people around, takin' pictures, sendin' threats! Fuck you think this is? Ain't shit sweet, nigga! I gotcho money, a'ight? Tell me where you want it and it's gon' get there. But ain't no more business between us after this."

"What if I told you I don't want the money?" King eased forward, interlacing his fingers under his chin as if he were praying. "In fact, what if I gave you *another* twenty-five blocks and two hundred fifty thousand cash for just *one* more deal? What would you say to that?"

I fell back in my chair, crossed my arms, and gazed at King Royce in disbelief. "Man, do you want the money or not?" I asked.

"No. What I want to do is pay you twenty-five more kilos and a quarter of a million dollars to blow a guy's brains out. I'll give you the dope and the cash up front, but if you try to fuck me over I'm coming after you and your little ladies over there. That I can promise."

I sat and stared at him for close to a minute, listening to the many conversations all around us but hearing none of them.

Finally, I leaned forward and said, "A'ight, who is it?"

Chapter 55

I paid Treecy a thousand dollars to cancel her and Momma's shopping plans, then followed them to their Drake Street home while Bubbles drove to her mother's place to drop off Ra'Mya. I dropped another thousand to Baby James, a TVL who managed all the dealings on Momma's block, and minutes later, an eight-man team of ambitious young Vice Lords were posted across the street from Momma's building with guns in the bushes and mugs on their faces.

I cruised up and down 16th Street for a while afterwards, smoking blunt after blunt and banging Chief Keef's "Bang 2" mixtape, trying to focus on the barely-dressed girls who were walking around enjoying the hot summer day.

But King Royce's offer was all I could think about.

Why did he want Cup dead? What had Cup done to get that kind of money put on his head? Reesie Cup was chief of the Traveling Vice Lords in my neighborhood. He had gotten rich in the dope game long before he'd started opening clubs all over the city. Now he was hardly even in the city, because now he had clubs all over the country. He was the only nigga in the hood pushing Ferraris, Bentleys, Lamborghinis, and just about every other car with a $200,000+ price tag. Every time he came through, it was a party… and he always brought the party to the house he owned on 15th and Trumbull.

The house was right next to the one Kisha and I had been living in for the past few weeks.

I shook away the thoughts and turned up the music.

'Pull off in that foreign, sker-sker-sker, she thought she seen a beast A nigga think I'm goin', Ha-Ha-Ha, I got my thing wit' me
The Glo gang known for glowin', Ha-Ha, all us got a thing apiece Seein' us she go, 'Ahaha', but you never seen the piece
I'm high off this earth, boy, I'm higher than Jesus be Comin' on my turf, boy, you gon' need a Jesus piece...'

I turned the volume back down, and then shut the music off completely, realizing that Chief Keef was the wrong nigga to be listening to when I was already contemplating murder.

I stopped on Trumbull and collected the cash from my workers. They had doled out two ounces of crack to the fiends, and I got $1,000 off each ounce. Lil Mark, my best worker, asked for a ride home so he could get something to eat. He got in the passenger seat with his head down. He was only fourteen, skinny as can be with light skin and dreadlocks that stretched halfway down his face. A loyal TVL, he was born and raised in our Holy City neighborhood. I'd known him since before I was his age, had gone to Dvorak High School with his older brother Tommy Lord.

Tommy had gotten himself killed last year, shot in the head while leaving some girl's house in a Breed neighborhood. We were still at war with the Breeds about that.

"Fuck wrong witchoo, lil nigga?" I clamped a palm atop his head and shook it fiercely. "Put that seatbelt on. Why you gotcha head all down? What's the matter? Gotcha lil heart broke by a thot?"

"Never dat, joe. You know I ain't never tweakin' off no thotties." Lil Mark let out a heavy breath as he secured his seatbelt. "It's them pussy ass Breeds on 13th. They chased me off the school bus yesterday. Nigga named Boony shot at me. We went over there this mornin' and tried to find 'em.

Wasn't nobody outside." He lifted his head and regarded me with fearful eyes. "I don't wanna die like my brother died. On Neal, joe, I'ma body one o'dem niggas 'fore I let 'em kill me."

"You strapped up now?" I was cruising down Trumbull, getting ready to make a right onto 15th.

"Yeah, I'm strapped. Ceno let me hold the Mac," Lil Mark said. He dug in his baggy jeans and pulled out a black steel Mack-11 with a 50- round clip hanging from the bottom of it.

"Where the nigga Boony live?" I asked.

"Right off 13th and Christiana. But he really be over there where you used to live on oTroy. His lil thottie, Melissa, stays in that red house, so the Breeds be chillin' at her spot wit' Boony."

I stomped on the gas and turned the music back on, zipping the heavy SUV up 15th Street, braking at every corner and swinging my head from left to right before speeding off again. It was difficult driving with only one eye. Ra'Mya had a point.

Veering left onto Kedzie, I took the Glock from my hip, ejected the 16-round magazine, and slipped in the 30-rounder.

"We goin' over there now?" Lil Mark asked.

"Don't freeze up if we catch this nigga," was my reply.

"Haaaa. I'll never freeze up. On Neal, I'm bangin' if he out here, wait and see."

I didn't have to wait long.

Lil Mark grabbed my arm as I was passing the convenience store on 13th and Kedzie. "That's him, Lord. That's Boony right there." He pointed and I caught a glimpse of the tall, dark skinned teen as I swerved onto 13th and brought my big Suburban to a near-screeching halt. Boony was walking out of the store with his hand lost inside a bag of barbeque Ruffles potato chips. He had on a black White Sox cap over a white tee and jeans.

Lil Mark flung his door open and jumped out. He ran up on Boony, who had his head tilted back, pouring what was left of the Ruffles into his mouth.

Boony never saw what hit him. The Mack-11 boomed and rattled and flashed in Lil Mark's hands. A line of bullets punched holes in Boony's neck and face. Then Lil Mark stood over him and painted his chest red.

Chapter 56

Clad in a costly Armani suit with a diamond Audemars watch dangling from his left wrist and a black bottle of Bel Air Rosé gripped snugly in his right hand, Reesie Cup descended the steps of his Gulfstream 5 ahead of his comely new assistant, the beautiful, caramel-hued Lashay Cooper.

She was tall and slender, and she possessed one of the sexiest walks Cup had ever seen. He'd seen her chatting with one of the dancers at his strip club two days prior. After walking over and introducing himself, he'd told her about the recent firing of his former personal assistant and that he was looking for someone to fill the position. He interviewed and hired her the following morning, $100 an hour, 60 hours a week. Today was her first day on the job. They had been in Atlanta at an important business meeting for most of the morning, and had just landed at Chicago's Midway airport.

There were three long, shiny, black Escalades and a matte black Mercedes Maybach 62 Landaulet waiting next to the jet. A short black man in a chauffeur's uniform stood beside the Maybach's open rear passenger door. He shut the door after Cup and Shay climbed in. For a minute, Shay watched as several of Cup's male assistants flitted out of the SUVs to fetch the luggage from inside the private jet.

"Does everyone get paid $100 an hour?" Shay asked suddenly. She was already overwhelmed by his affluent lifestyle. He'd surprised her in his office that morning when he had a group of stylists wheel in four racks of ridiculously expensive dresses, bags, and heels, all for her. Now she was sitting beside him, wearing a black Marchesa dress, four-inch Gucci heels, and a large Gucci shoulder bag that was worth more than her Mustang.

"Not everybody is worth $100 an hour," replied Cup. He turned up the bubbly and took a full swallow while tapping and sliding the thumb of his other hand across his iPhone 5's screen. "Some get less, some get more, you know. Work ethic is what it's all about with me. Respect me and my business by working like a slave, and I promise, you and your family will eat like kings and queens. Get lazy like a king and you'll be returning to whatever slave wages your former employer paid you. Here"—he handed her his smartphone—"call Chubb and tell him to bring the barbeque grills to the house on Trumbull, like we did last summer. And copy my list of contacts into your phone. You need to know everyone I know. It'll be easier that way, trust me. Oh, and tell Chubb to spend a few thousand dollars on food so everybody can eat. Then call Nona at the Visionary Lounge and tell her to load up two hundred bottles of Ace of Spades. I want them brought to 1528 South Trumbull Avenue."

Shay located Chubb and Nona in Cup's contacts list and made the calls, continuing to peruse the list as she delivered his demands. Her eyes widened in shock at a few of the names. There were names of several prominent black celebrities. Shay hoped working for Cup would allow her the opportunity to one day meet them.

"So how'd you and Bubbles meet?" Cup suddenly asked.

Shay turned and offered Cup a questioning stare. "Please tell me you didn't hire me to get the scoop on my girl."

"No. Absolutely not. I saw you and her talking the other night, that's all. I just wondered where you knew her from. She used to date this rapper that I'm not too fond of, and last year Nona overheard her gossiping to him about me on the same day the Feds indicted over forty of my friends. I thought about firing her then, but she's the top-earning dancer at Redbone's, you know. What's good for business is good for me. But what I don't need is a personal assistant revealing what goes on with me to her gossiping friend. Understand what I'm saying? My business is my business. I'd like to keep it that way."

"For twenty-four thousand dollars a month, my lips are sealed. Bubbles is my girl and all, but I'm not losing my job over her, especially not this job. The most I've ever made before is $13 an hour as a prison guard. If you want me to stop associating with Bubbles, I'll do it. All you have to do is give me the word."

Cup cracked a smile. With his light brown complexion and gleaming bald head, Shay considered him incredibly attractive.

"No need for that sort of move," he said, taking another sip from his black bottle. "Just... keep her close. Let me know if she ever says anything you think I should know. If she mentions Bulletface, or Alexus Costilla, it will benefit you greatly to tell me immediately." He paused to look at his diamond watch. "Hurry up and get those contacts copied into your phone. And feel free to take the rest of the day off if you want. You'll still be paid for a full day's work. I'm turning down on the corporate world for a couple hours to turn up with my people on 15th and Trumbull and I wouldn't feel comfortable having you there with me. A lot of people have been getting shot in my old neighborhood. I wouldn't want you around that kind of environment."

"Too late. I already experienced violence a few weeks ago when my twin was killed. And you're right; I don't want to be around that." Shay turned and looked out her window as the Maybach convertible floated out of the airport behind the Escalades. She felt Cup's eyes on the side of her face, but for nearly a full minute she ignored him and thought about her twin sister's unsolved murder.

The homicide detective in charge of investigating the triple homicide had told Lashay everything he knew, and didn't know, about the case. Some lunatic had rear-ended her sister's boyfriend's car, causing a terrible crash that severely injured Cashay, her boyfriend, and a male friend of his. Then all three of them had suffered gunshots to the head. The only evidence the killer left was a bunch of spent shells and a scratch of orange paint on the bumper of the boyfriend's car. The two male victims were reputed Chicago gang members with too many enemies to list. Without an eyewitness, no arrests were possible.

Shay sighed, wiped a single tear from her left eye, and went back to copying Cup's contacts into her phone. She had to stay busy. It was the only way she could keep from sobbing over Cashay.

"Sorry to hear about your sister," Cup said.

"Thanks."

"Did it happen here in Chicago?"

"It was in Michigan City, Indiana, our hometown. That's where we were staying. We only visit Chicago to hang out with Bubbles. And my sister had another girl she kicked it with on thirteenth and Troy. I believe her name's Patrice, or Latrice... something like that." "Big Mike's daughter? Treecy?"

Shay frowned, "Big Mike?"

"Yeah. Somebody killed him about a month ago."

"Does he have a son?"

Cup nodded. "Lil Mikey. He's one of the younger Vice Lords. I hear he's been getting money lately, and shooting everything in his way. Wild lil nigga. I've known him since he was a kid."

Nodding her head thoughtfully, Shay set her eyes on her phone and left them there for a long moment. She thought of the orange scratch of paint on her sister's boyfriend's car... and remembered the orange paint job on the Chevy Caprice that had been parked in front of Bubbles' place on the evening of her sister's funeral.

Suddenly, she was racing up her own contacts list. She stopped on the name 'Bubbles' and dialed the number.

Chapter 57

"King Royce asked me to kill your boss; said he'd pay me another twenty-five bricks and a quarter million cash."

"He wants you to kill *Cup*?"

"I know. That's what I said. Nigga got me fucked up. What I look like killin' a Lord when I'm a Vice Lord? And of all people, he asked me to body *Cup*. Every nigga in Holy City would be at my head if I killed Cup."

"If he dies, half of Lawndale will be out of work, including me."

Bubbles bit down on her thumbnail and shook her head. We were on her living room sofa, and Lil Mark was standing at the large front window, peeking through the blinds, holding the Mac-11 submachine gun at his side.

"Your little friend is making me nervous," Bubbles whispered, jumping up as her phone began to ring from somewhere inside her bedroom.

I cast a suggestive stare at her massive, undulating ass as Bubbles walked around the sofa and into her bedroom. Then I turned to Lil Mark and saw that he too had been watching Bubbles leave the room.

"You hit the jackpot wit' her, bruh. She got the fattest ass on earth," Lil Mark said. He was already peeking out through the blinds again.

"Man, sit the fuck down somewhere. Get away from that window." I got up. "Come on; let's go in the kitchen. You still hungry?"

"Hell yeah." Lil Mark followed me to the kitchen with his eyes on his phone. "I think I gave Boony 'bout thirty of 'em. You see my shoes? Got blood all over these muhfuckas."

"Stop talkin' about that shit," I snapped, pausing in front of the large stainless steel refrigerator. "Keep that to yourself, lil homie. Take it to the grave witchoo. Real niggas don't talk about bodies anyway. That'll get you jammed up quick."

I opened the refrigerator, found a Glad bowl full of leftover pizza, and warmed it up in the microwave.

"I only want a slice," Lil Mark said, eyes still glued to the screen of his smartphone. "Everybody on Facebook sayin' Cup throwin' another barbeque on Trumbull, like he did last year. You know it's gon' be all kinda food over there. Damn, bruh, you *gotta* drop me off on Trumbull *ASAP*, joe. It's gon' be about a hun'ed *bad* bitches out there."

Leaning back on the counter, I bit into a slice of pizza and studied Lil Mark's excited expression as he thumbed his way down his Facebook page. *'What a coincidence,'* I thought. *'Cup comes to town on the same day I get offered an irresistible deal to kill him.'*

I shook my head incredulously and finished off the slice of pizza. Bubbles walked in with her hands on her hips. She gave me an odd stare.

"Fuck you lookin' at?" I asked. "I'm not sure," she drably replied.

Lil Mark chuckled once but didn't look up from his phone. "Mikey, can I have a word with you in my bedroom?" Bubbles spun around and left the kitchen before I could reply.

I checked my Rolex for the time—4:14pm—then followed Bubbles to the bedroom. I sat at the foot of the bed. She muted the wall- mounted flat-screen television, shut the door, and rested her shoulder against it. Crossing her arms, she regarded me with the same odd stare she'd given me in the kitchen.

"What?" I said.

She sighed. "Were you involved in what happened to a girl named Cashay Cooper? She used to hang out with your sister."

My heart skipped a beat. I gazed at Bubbles and didn't say a word. *'How did she find out?'* I wondered.

I looked at my watch again.

Bubbles let out another sigh, and for an infinite moment we just stared at each other.

Finally, she said, "Where is that Chevy you were driving the day we met? If you had anything to do with Cashay getting killed, you need to get rid of that car. Her sister just called me talking about calling the police and getting your car searched for evidence, something about some paint. She was with Cup when she called, said she's his new personal assistant."

I put my head down and started thinking. I hadn't driven the Caprice since my release from the hospital. It was sitting in the trash-littered vacant lot next to Kisha's house on Trumbull.

"King Royce is supposed to be delivering that payment in forty-five minutes," I said, changing the subject. "We're meeting up at five o'clock, in the alley on Trumbull."

"Wait a minute." Bubbles got off the door and her hands went to her hips. "So, you mean to tell me that you're actually going to accept the payment to kill Cup? I'm sorry, but you can't kill my damn boss."

"I'm not touchin' Cup." I looked up at Bubbles. "I'm just gon' get that shit and keep it. Fuck that nigga Royce. I'll send Momma and Treecy to Texas. Momma's sister lives down there. Then you can tell me where to find Royce, and I'll body his ass."

Bubbles sucked her teeth and shook her head. "I've never been to King's house, okay? I just know him from the club."

"So what? All you gotta do is ask around. Sombody'll know where he lives."

There was another suck of the teeth. I heard Lil Mark's phone ring in the kitchen. From somewhere, blocks away, police sirens shrieked.

"I'll think about it, Mikey. But you and that crazy lookin' little boy you got in my kitchen need to be leaving so I can get a few hours of sleep. You can come back by yourself, but I don't wanna see any of your friends in my house ever again. Family only, baby."

"I can respect that," I said, getting up as she pulled open the door. "But, you know, the Travelers are my family. I'm a Vice Lord, baby. All you gon' see is Vice Lords around me. I trust them niggas wit' my life."

"Boy, please. This is Chicago; you can't trust nobody."

Chapter 58

I was nervous about driving the Suburban after using it to flee the scene of Boony's murder. Lil Mark, who was sitting next to me with the Mac-11 on his lap, chewing his fingernails to shreds and flicking his eyes in every direction, exacerbated my nervousness tenfold. With Chief Keef's "Smash" blaring from my speakers, I reclined my seat a bit and accelerated up 16th Street, on my way to Trumbull Avenue.

Lil Mark suddenly reached forward and lowered the volume on my

music. "Can't hear myself think," he muttered.

I almost checked him for fucking with my music. But he had the perilous gun on his lap, and he was obviously more nervous than I was, so I let it go.

"Fuck you thinkin' 'bout?" I asked.

"That phone call I got when you was in the bedroom with that bitch."

"What phone call? Who was it?"

Lil Mark shook his head and got quiet, then turned and looked out his window as I made a slow left turn onto Trumbull, drove halfway down the block, and parked in front of Kisha's place.

I pulled out my cell phone and tried to come up with a way to end my relationship with Kisha. Plain and simple, I now wanted nothing more than to be with Bubbles. Kisha had to go.

Out of the corner of my eye, I saw Lil Mark pick up the Mac-11, but I paid it no mind... until the gun started booming and flashing and jerking in his hands.

***

Mikey reached for Lil Mark's gun and caught several bullets through his hands, wrists, and forearms. He made a frantic attempt at lifting his legs to kick at Lil Mark and got his jeans filled with holes. Lil Mark raised the gun, put three holes in Mikey's shirt, then pushed open his door and leapt out, running around to the passenger side of the white Panamera that had just pulled up alongside the Suburban.

Lil Mark got in beside Lil Cholly, who stared into the SUV at Mikey's blood-soaked figure before racing away in the Porsche.

Cholly stopped in an alleyway two blocks over. Lil Mark tossed the Mac-11 out his window and watched it skid under a dumpster.

"You sure he was dead?" Cholly asked.

"Hell yeah, joe. He ain't comin' back from that."

"Did you shoot him in the face?"

Lil Mark hesitated. "Yeah," he muttered weakly.

"You sure?"

"I said yeah, nigga." Lil Mark's voice strengthened. "Man stop askin' me so many questions. I know how to kill a muhfucka. I just whacked a nigga 'bout two hours ago."

Lil Cholly was chuckling as he veered out of the alley. "Just makin' sure, lil homie. Mikey ain't the kinda nigga you can just shoot and let live. He was gangsta like his daddy was."

"So what? Ain't no nigga bigger than this mob. Fuck that nigga and his daddy. I'm a gangsta's son, too."

Lock Down Publications and Ca$h Presents Assisted Publishing Packages

Due to an increase in the price of services we have increased our prices. The prices below reflect the price increase as of 11/1/24.

BASIC PACKAGE $699 Editing Cover Design Formatting	UPGRADED PACKAGE $1000 Typing Editing Cover Design Formatting Upload eBooks to Amazon Upload Paperback to Amazon
ADVANCE PACKAGE $1,400 Typing Editing (line editing/content) Cover Design Formatting Copyright Registration Proofreading Upload eBooks to Amazon Upload Paperback to Amazon	LDP SUPREME PACKAGE $1,700 Typing Editing (line editing/content) Cover Design Formatting Copyright Registration Proofreading Set up Amazon Account Upload eBooks to Amazon Upload Paperback to Amazon Advertise on LDP's Amazon and Facebook Page

***Other services available upon request.
Additional charges may apply

Lock Down Publications
P.O. Box 944
Stockbridge, GA 30281-9998
Phone: 470 303-9761
Email: lockdownpublications@gmail.com

Submission Guideline

Submit the first three chapters of your completed manuscript to ldpsubmissions@gmail.com. In the subject line add **Your Book's Title**. The manuscript must be in a Word Doc file and sent as an attachment. Document should be in Times New Roman, double spaced, and in size 12 font. Also, provide your synopsis and full contact information. If sending multiple submissions, they must each be in a separate email.

Have a story but no way to send it electronically? You can still submit to LDP/Ca$h Presents. Send in the first three chapters, written or typed, of your completed manuscript to:

LDP: Submissions Dept
P.O. Box 944
Stockbridge, GA 30281-9998

DO NOT send original manuscript. Must be a duplicate. Provide your synopsis and a cover letter containing your full contact information.

Thanks for considering LDP and Ca$h Presents.

NEW RELEASES

BLOODLINE OF A SAVAGE 1,2&3
THESE VICIOUS STREETS 1,2&3
RELENTLESS GOON
RELENTLESS GOON 2
BY PRINCE A. TAUHID

THE BUTTERFLY MAFIA 1-3
BY FUMIYA PAYNE

A THUG'S STREET PRINCESS 1,2&3
BY MEESHA

CITY OF SMOKE 1& 2
BY MOLOTTI

STEPPERS 1,2&3
THE REAL BADDIES OF CHI-RAQ
BY KING RIO

THE LANE 1&2
BY KEN-KEN SPENCE

THUG OF SPADES 1,2&3
LOVE IN THE TRENCHES 2
CORNER BOY CHRONICLES
BY COREY ROBINSON

TIL DEATH 3
BY ARYANNA

THE BIRTH OF A GANGSTER 4
BY DELMONT PLAYER

A GANGSTA'S SON | KING RIO

PRODUCT OF THE STREETS 1&2
BY DEMOND "MONEY" ANDERSON

NO TIME FOR ERROR
BY KEESE

MONEY HUNGRY DEMONS 1,2&3
BY TRANAY ADAMS

HUNGRY FOR MONEY 1&2
BY SLIMBOS

A THUGGISH PASSION
KILLAZ ON STANDBY 1&2
LAND OF DA HOOLIGANZ 1,2&3
FRESH OFF DA PORCH
BY IRA B.

COUNTDOWN OF A KILLA 1&2
GUNS DOWN, BOTTOMS UP 1&2
SEX, MURDA AND GOD
BY LO-LIFE

THE LEVEL UP 1&2
BY LUXURY KING

FO'EVA ROLLIN' 1&2
BY ASSA RAYMOND BAKER

HUB CITY MENACE 1&2
BY J. WHITE

KILLA CREW
DYING FOR LIKES
BY ARYANNA

IF YOU CROSS ME ONCE 6
ANGEL 5
By Anthony Fields

IMMA DIE BOUT MINE 5
By Aryanna

A THUGS STREET PRINCESS 3
EMBRACING THE LOVE OF A BOSS
By Meesha

PRODUCT OF THE STREETS 3
By Demond Money Anderson

STANDING ON HER BUSINESS
BY DG SANTANA

GET IT IN SLUGS 1&2
B. STALLS

CORNER BOYS 2
By Corey Robinson

THE MURDER QUEENS 6&7
By Michael Gallon

CITY OF SMOKE 3
By Molotti

CONFESSIONS OF A DOPEBOY
By Nicholas Lock

TENDER
BY KHUFU

THA TAKEOVER
By Keith Chandler

BETRAYAL OF A G 2
By Ray Vinci

CRIME BOSS 4
By Playa Ray

Coming Soon from Lock Down Publications/Ca$h Presents

RAN OFF ON THE PLUG 2 by **PAPER BOI RARI**
STREET REDEMPTION by **TONY DANIELS**
SAVAGE FAMILY EMPIRE by **PRINCE TAUHID**
BAD BITCHES WIT' GUNZ by **DIESEL**
THE SINGLE LADIES by **DIESEL**
COKE BY THE TRUCKLOAD by **DIESEL**
PROBLEM SOLVED by **DIESEL**
TIPPIN' THE SCALES by **DIESEL**
OPPS CRY TOO by **SAYNOMORE**
A GANGSTA'S KARMA by **FLAME**

AVAILABLE NOW

RESTRAINING ORDER 1 & 2
By **CA$H & Coffee**

LOVE KNOWS NO BOUNDARIES 1-3
By **Coffee**

RAISED AS A GOON I, II, III & IV
BRED BY THE SLUMS I, II, III
BLAST FOR ME I & II
ROTTEN TO THE CORE I II III
A BRONX TALE I, II, III
DUFFLE BAG CARTEL I II III IV V VI
HEARTLESS GOON I II III IV V
A SAVAGE DOPEBOY I II
DRUG LORDS I II III
CUTTHROAT MAFIA I II
KING OF THE TRENCHES
By **Ghost**

LAY IT DOWN I & II
LAST OF A DYING BREED I II
BLOOD STAINS OF A SHOTTA I & II III
By **Jamaica**

LOYAL TO THE GAME I II III
LIFE OF SIN I, II III
By **TJ & Jelissa**

IF LOVING HIM IS WRONG…I & II
LOVE ME EVEN WHEN IT HURTS I II III
By **Jelissa**

A GANGSTA'S SON | KING RIO

PUSH IT TO THE LIMIT
By **Bre' Hayes**

BLOODY COMMAS I & II
SKI MASK CARTEL I, II & III
KING OF NEW YORK I II, III IV V
RISE TO POWER I II III
COKE KINGS I II III IV V
BORN HEARTLESS I II III IV
KING OF THE TRAP I II
By **T.J. Edwards**

WHEN THE STREETS CLAP BACK I & II III
THE HEART OF A SAVAGE I II III IV
MONEY MAFIA I II
LOYAL TO THE SOIL I II III
By **Jibril Williams**

A DISTINGUISHED THUG STOLE MY HEART I - III
LOVE SHOULDN'T HURT I II III IV
RENEGADE BOYS 1-4
PAID IN KARMA 1-3
SAVAGE STORMS 1-3
AN UNFORESEEN LOVE 1-3
BABY, I'M WINTERTIME COLD 1-3
A THUG'S STREET PRINCESS 1&2
By **Meesha**

CUM FOR ME 1-8
An LDP Erotica Collaboration

BLOOD OF A BOSS 1-5
SHADOWS OF THE GAME
TRAP BASTARD
By **Askari**

A GANGSTER'S CODE 1-3
A GANGSTER'S SYN 1-3
THE SAVAGE LIFE 1-3
CHAINED TO THE STREETS 1-3
BLOOD ON THE MONEY 1-3
A GANGSTA'S PAIN 1-3
BEAUTIFUL LIES AND UGLY TRUTHS
CHURCH IN THESE STREETS
By **J-Blunt**

THE STREETS BLEED MURDER 1-3
THE HEART OF A GANGSTA 1-3
By **Jerry Jackson**

WHEN A GOOD GIRL GOES BAD
By **Adrienne**

THE COST OF LOYALTY 1-3
By **Kweli**

BRIDE OF A HUSTLA 1-3
THE FETTI GIRLS 1-3
CORRUPTED BY A GANGSTA 1-4
BLINDED BY HIS LOVE
THE PRICE YOU PAY FOR LOVE 1-3
DOPE GIRL MAGIC 1-3
By **Destiny Skai**

A KINGPIN'S AMBITION
A KINGPIN'S AMBITION II
I MURDER FOR THE DOUGH
By **Ambitious**

A DOPEBOY'S PRAYER
By **Eddie "Wolf" Lee**

TRUE SAVAGE 1-7
DOPE BOY MAGIC 1-3
MIDNIGHT CARTEL 1-3
CITY OF KINGZ 1&2
NIGHTMARE ON SILENT AVE
THE PLUG OF LIL MEXICO 1&2
CLASSIC CITY
By **Chris Green**

LOVE & CHASIN' PAPER
By **Qay Crockett**

THE KING CARTEL 1-3
By **Frank Gresham**

THESE NIGGAS AIN'T LOYAL 1-3
By **Nikki Tee**

GANGSTA SHYT 1-3
By **CATO**

THE ULTIMATE BETRAYAL
By **Phoenix**

BOSS'N UP 1-3
By **Royal Nicole**

I LOVE YOU TO DEATH
By **Destiny J**

BROOKLYN HUSTLAZ
By **Boogsy Morina**

GANGSTA CITY
By **Teddy Duke**

TO DIE IN VAIN
SINS OF A HUSTLA
By **ASAD**

I RIDE FOR MY HITTA
I STILL RIDE FOR MY HITTA
By **Misty Holt**

A GANGSTER'S REVENGE 1-4
THE BOSS MAN'S DAUGHTERS 1-5
A SAVAGE LOVE 1&2
BAE BELONGS TO ME 1&2
A HUSTLER'S DECEIT 1-3
WHAT BAD BITCHES DO 1-3
SOUL OF A MONSTER 1-3
KILL ZONE
A DOPE BOY'S QUEEN 1-3
TIL DEATH 1-3
IMMA DIE BOUT MINE 1-5
By **Aryanna**

BROOKLYN ON LOCK 1 & 2
By **Sonovia**

A DRUG KING AND HIS DIAMOND 1-3
A DOPEMAN'S RICHES
HER MAN, MINE'S TOO 1&2
CASH MONEY HO'S
THE WIFEY I USED TO BE 1&2
PRETTY GIRLS DO NASTY THINGS
By **Nicole Goosby**

THE STREETS ARE CALLING
By **Duquie Wilson**

LIPSTICK KILLAH 1-3
CRIME OF PASSION 1-3
FRIEND OR FOE 1-3
By **Mimi**

TRAPHOUSE KING 1-3
KINGPIN KILLAZ 1-3
STREET KINGS 1&2
PAID IN BLOOD 1&2
CARTEL KILLAZ 1-3
DOPE GODS 1&2
By **Hood Rich**

STEADY MOBBN' 1-3
THE STREETS STAINED MY SOUL 1-3
By **Marcellus Allen**

WHO SHOT YA 1-3
SON OF A DOPE FIEND 1-4
HEAVEN GOT A GHETTO 1&2
SKI MASK MONEY 1&2
By **Renta**

GORILLAZ IN THE BAY 1-4
TEARS OF A GANGSTA 1/&2
3X KRAZY 1&2
STRAIGHT BEAST MODE 1&2
By **DE'KARI**

TRIGGADALE 1-3
MURDA WAS THE CASE 1-3
By **Elijah R. Freeman**

MARRIED TO A BOSS 1-3
By **Destiny Skai & Chris Green**

SLAUGHTER GANG 1-3
RUTHLESS HEART 1-3
By **Willie Slaughter**

GOD BLESS THE TRAPPERS 1-3
THESE SCANDALOUS STREETS 1-3
FEAR MY GANGSTA 1-5
THESE STREETS DON'T LOVE NOBODY 1-2
BURY ME A G 1-5
A GANGSTA'S EMPIRE 1-4
THE DOPEMAN'S BODYGAURD 1&2
THE REALEST KILLAZ 1-3
THE LAST OF THE OGS 1-3
By **Tranay Adams**

KINGZ OF THE GAME 1-7
CRIME BOSS 1-4
By **Playa Ray**

FUK SHYT
By **Blakk Diamond**

DON'T F#CK WITH MY HEART 1&2
By **Linnea**

ADDICTED TO THE DRAMA 1-3
IN THE ARM OF HIS BOSS
By **Jamila**

LOYALTY AIN'T PROMISED 1&2
By **Keith Williams**

FOREVER GANGSTA 1&2
GLOCKS ON SATIN SHEETS 1&2
By **Adrian Dulan**

YAYO 1-4
A SHOOTER'S AMBITION 1&2
BRED IN THE GAME
By **S. Allen**

TRAP GOD 1-3
RICH $AVAGE 1-3
MONEY IN THE GRAVE 1-3
CARTEL MONEY
By **Martell Troublesome Bolden**

TOE TAGZ 1-4
LEVELS TO THIS SHYT 1&2
IT'S JUST ME AND YOU
By **Ah'Million**

KINGPIN DREAMS 1-3
RAN OFF ON DA PLUG
By **Paper Boi Rari**

THE STREETS MADE ME 1-3
By **Larry D. Wright**

CONFESSIONS OF A GANGSTA 1-4
CONFESSIONS OF A JACKBOY 1-3
CONFESSIONS OF A HITMAN
By **Nicholas Lock**

I'M NOTHING WITHOUT HIS LOVE
SINS OF A THUG
TO THE THUG I LOVED BEFORE
A GANGSTA SAVED XMAS
IN A HUSTLER I TRUST
By **Monet Dragun**

A GANGSTA'S SON | KING RIO

QUIET MONEY 1-3
THUG LIFE 1-3
EXTENDED CLIP 1&2
A GANGSTA'S PARADISE
By **Trai'Quan**

CAUGHT UP IN THE LIFE 1-3
THE STREETS NEVER LET GO 1-3
By **Robert Baptiste**

NEW TO THE GAME 1-3
MONEY, MURDER & MEMORIES 1-3
By **Malik D. Rice**

THE LIFE OF A HOOD STAR
By **Ca$h & Rashia Wilson**

THE STREETS WILL NEVER CLOSE 1-4
By **K'ajji**

LIFE OF A SAVAGE 1-4
A GANGSTA'S QUR'AN 1-4
MURDA SEASON 1-3
GANGLAND CARTEL 1-3
CHI'RAQ GANGSTAS 1-4
KILLERS ON ELM STREET 1-3
JACK BOYZ N DA BRONX 1-3
A DOPEBOY'S DREAM 1-3
JACK BOYS VS DOPE BOYS 1-3
COKE GIRLZ
COKE BOYS
SOSA GANG 1&2
BRONX SAVAGES
BODYMORE KINGPINS
BLOOD OF A GOON
By **Romell Tukes**

CREAM 2-3
THE STREETS WILL TALK
By **Yolanda Moore**

CONCRETE KILLA 1-3
VICIOUS LOYALTY 1-3
By **Kingpen**

THE ULTIMATE SACRIFICE 1-6
KHADIFI
IF YOU CROSS ME ONCE 1-5
ANGEL 1-4
IN THE BLINK OF AN EYE
By **Anthony Fields**

NIGHTMARES OF A HUSTLA 1-3
BLOOD AND GAMES 1&2
By **King Dream**

HARD AND RUTHLESS 1&2
MOB TOWN 251
THE BILLIONAIRE BENTLEYS 1-3
REAL G'S MOVE IN SILENCE
By **Von Diesel**

MOB TIES 1-7
SOUL OF A HUSTLER, HEART OF A KILLER 1-3
GORILLAZ IN THE TRENCHES
By **SayNoMore**

BODYMORE MURDERLAND 1-3
THE BIRTH OF A GANGSTER 1-4
By **Delmont Player**

FOR THE LOVE OF A BOSS 1&2
By **C. D. Blue**

KILLA KOUNTY 1-5
By **Khufu**

MOBBED UP 1-4
THE BRICK MAN 1-5
THE COCAINE PRINCESS 1-10
STEPPERS 1-3
SUPER GREMLIN 1-4
By **King Rio**

MONEY GAME 1&2
By **Smoove Dolla**

A GANGSTA'S KARMA 1-4
By **FLAME**

KING OF THE TRENCHES 1-3
By **GHOST & TRANAY ADAMS**

QUEEN OF THE ZOO 1&2
By **Black Migo**

GRIMEY WAYS 1-3
BETRAYAL OF A G
By **Ray Vinci**

XMAS WITH AN ATL SHOOTER
By **Ca$h & Destiny Skai**

KING KILLA 1&2
By **Vincent "Vitto" Holloway**

BETRAYAL OF A THUG 1&2
By **Fre$h**

A GANGSTA'S SON | KING RIO

THE MURDER QUEENS 1-6
By **Michael Gallon**

FOR THE LOVE OF BLOOD 1-4
By **Jamel Mitchell**

HOOD CONSIGLIERE 1&2
NO TIME FOR ERROR
By **Keese**

PROTÉGÉ OF A LEGEND 1&2
LOVE IN THE TRENCHES 1&2
By **Corey Robinson**

THE PLUG'S RUTHLESS DAUGHTER 1&2
By **Tony Daniels**

BORN IN THE GRAVE 1-3
CRIME PAYS 1&2
By **Self Made Tay**

MOAN IN MY MOUTH
By **XTASY**

TORN BETWEEN A GANGSTER AND A
GENTLEMAN
By **J-BLUNT & Miss Kim**

HERE TODAY GONE TOMORROW 1&2
By **Fly Rock**

PILLOW PRINCESS
By **S. Hawkins**

SANCTIFIED AND HORNY
by **XTASY**

WOMEN LIE MEN LIE 1-4
FIFTY SHADES OF SNOW 1-3
STACK BEFORE YOU SPLURGE
GIRLS FALL LIKE DOMINOES
NAÏVE TO THE STREETS
By **ROY MILLIGAN**

LOYALTY IS EVERYTHING 1-3
CITY OF SMOKE 1&2
By **Molotti**

THE BUTTERFLY MAFIA 1-4
SALUTE MY SAVAGERY 1&2
By **Fumiya Payne**

THE LANE 1&2
By **Ken-Ken Spence**

THE PUSSY TRAP 1-5
By **Nene Capri**

DIRTY DNA
By **Blaque**

BOOKS BY LDP'S CEO, CA$H

TRUST IN NO MAN
TRUST IN NO MAN 2
TRUST IN NO MAN 3
BONDED BY BLOOD
SHORTY GOT A THUG
THUGS CRY
THUGS CRY 2
THUGS CRY 3
TRUST NO BITCH
TRUST NO BITCH 2
TRUST NO BITCH 3
TIL MY CASKET DROPS
RESTRAINING ORDER
RESTRAINING ORDER 2
IN LOVE WITH A CONVICT
LIFE OF A HOOD STAR
XMAS WITH AN ATL SHOOTER